FORECLOSURE GOTHIC

FORECLOSURE GOTHIC

HARRIS LAHTI

Astra House
New York

Astra House
A Division of Astra Publishing House
astrahouse.com
Printed in the United States of America

Library of Congress Cataloging-in-Publication Data

Names: Lahti, Harris, author.
Title: Foreclosure gothic / Harris Lahti.
Description: New York : Astra House, 2025. | Summary: "A multi-generational and deeply autobiographical gothic tale of Hollywood dreams and upstate New York reality"— Provided by publisher.
Identifiers: LCCN 2024052790 (print) | LCCN 2024052791 (ebook) | ISBN 9781662602825 (hardback) | ISBN 9781662602818 (ebook)
Subjects: LCGFT: Novels.
Classification: LCC PS3612.A45 F67 2025 (print) | LCC PS3612.A45 (ebook) | DDC 813/.6—dc23/eng/20250106
LC record available at https://lccn.loc.gov/2024052790
LC ebook record available at https://lccn.loc.gov/2024052791

First edition

10 9 8 7 6 5 4 3 2 1

Design by Alissa Theodor
The text is set in Sabon MT Std.
The titles are set in Real Vhs Font.

FORECLOSURE GOTHIC

CONTENTS

THIS ONLY ENDS ONE WAY

After two years of rejection, somehow, finally, Vic Greener lands an agent. Who lands him some real work: a national shampoo commercial. Which lands him some even realer work: a guest spot as this sociopathic cocaine-addict doctor on the popular daytime soap *Days of our Lives*.

More than once, he says, "You know how many houses I'd have to paint to earn that!?"

The script arrives late one night at his Oakwood apartment, along with a telegram from his agent that reads, "Break a leg at the taping. The writer/director loved your audition so much there's already talk of roping you into the murder plot."

Vic opens the script immediately, begins reading lines. He speaks them and paces. Tentatively, at first. Then, less so. At times, answering as the actress in the scene, his voice pitching high and low. At different volumes, in different accents. Until his neighbor starts pounding on the wall.

Preparations resume as soon as Vic wakes. *Today*, he thinks into the popcorn ceiling above his twin-size bed, *I'll go full method*. At the bathroom mirror, he slides the doctor's face over his face—what then occurs to him as a mask of ice, capable of only the most necessary human contortions, save the eyes. Those will remain permanently cold, he decides, marveling at himself in the bathroom mirror. At *this* doctor.

Vic steers this vehicle of success down to the Venice Board-walk, stopping off at the taqueria on the way—the one with the wall of signed headshots—where the doctor proceeds to order a veggie burrito with cilantro. Vic's never ordered one this way before (he hates cilantro). Nevertheless, the doctor tears the meal apart in a few hungry bites. Scraps of rice, beans, tortilla tumble down his chin to the table and tray. Before walking off, he glares at the aftermath. Then he leaves the mess for someone else to clean.

Throngs of pedestrians with neon-clad Rollerbladers weaving in and out of them. A distant boom box: synthesizers, a drum machine. A breakdancer doing a head spin on a flattened piece of cardboard. *Fucking breakdancers*, the doctor thinks. The doctor despises them, he finds, as well as most other things, namely recumbent bikes and small dogs.

The doctor curses at a homeless man.

The doctor ignores the greeting of a dolled-up old actress whose home Vic sprayed with paint last spring.

The doctor winks at a leather-tanned, bikinied woman. He holds his pinky up to the x-ray sun and grows a coke-spoon nail before his very eyes—

But there's something about the doctor's gait Vic can't get right. A straight line of paint his hand refuses to cut, a mold he can't bleach away. Would a wolflike bounce haunt his step? Or a serial killer's robot beeline? A pigeon toe from a traumatic childhood he couldn't quite hide?

Frustrated, Vic slides the doctor's face off, goes and sits at his usual spot: this concrete ledge off the boardwalk where he often comes to mine the endless parade of pedestrians for gestures he might incorporate into his craft.

Sure enough, an obese man in aviator sunglasses and an oversize Lakers T-shirt comes along, licking at a melting ice-cream cone. Suddenly, his face pinches, then relaxes. Then pinches again. He jerks his head back, sniffing in an attempt to ward off the incoming sneeze just long enough to lick away the melting edge of his ice-cream cone.

It's a valuable beat, Vic realizes. One he might consider incorporating into his doctor to dislodge the cocaine gunk that surely clings to the insides of his rusty nostrils. With a sniff, he jerks his head back. But the sniff feels too hard, the jerk too soft, and he must recalibrate. A little better now. Softer, truer to life this time. Not perfect. But getting there—

"Are you all right?" someone asks.

Vic shields his eyes and the figure of a slender woman clarifies— dirty moccasins, white leggings. An oversize black sweater hanging off one shoulder. Deep clavicles, a crooked bottom tooth. An upturned nose like a knuckle. Dark eyes and glossy raven hair.

With a long finger, she points at the space between his eyes. "I thought you were having a fit or something."

Vic laughs. "You could say that, I suppose. I was preparing for a role—this sociopathic doctor. Here, lookit." He slides the doctor's face on. Ice settling into his eyes, he jerks back his head and sniffs a couple of times. Then he slides the doctor's face off again. "See?" he says.

"I do," the woman says, and introduces herself: "Heather Roswell."

"Are you an actor, too?"

"You could say that," she says. "But you could say a lot of things. I travel—or I should say *traveled*—with this theater group. Until recently. Very recently. Highly experimental stuff. Improv, chanting, breathing. Orgone energy. You know, that type of thing."

To which, Vic admits that, no, he doesn't know about that type of thing and waits for her to elaborate. For stars to slide into her eyes as she identifies the theater group as a stepping stone to larger ambition. A mere exercise meant to keep her teeth sharp until she landed the role that'd change her life. A future she'd been all but promised by a handful of lauded auditions and close calls. One that'd justify all the shrimp puffs she'd passed out at catering jobs, all the exhaust fumes she'd huffed selling roses down on Hollywood Boulevard

But Heather says none of that. Instead, she brushes a smeared Mars-bar wrapper off the ledge and perches beside him. Where she begins studying the flow of pedestrians with a heightened attention that, for whatever reason, feels obscene to interrupt—

An oily weightlifter with tree-trunk arms.

A shopper bogged down with countless bags.

Another herd of neon-clad roller-bladers.

A seven-foot-tall man in a wooden warthog mask with tusks bent upward like a crown.

Side by side, they track these figures in silence, and more. So many more. Their attention overlapping and moving in tandem like two dolphins swimming in the wake of a boat. An intimacy sparking between them. A warmth that tickles at his bones.

"What's *your* backstory?" she says suddenly.

"No way. You first," he says.

"Not a chance."

And so, Vic tells her about upstate New York—growing up renovating foreclosed houses with a workaholic father. How that'd been a path he'd been fated to follow. Until (and of all things) a rave review in the local paper for a performance in a high school musical trained his sights on Hollywood. The years of rejection that followed. And how lately things have turned around for him—the agent, the national shampoo commercial, the promise of this guest spot.

Heather laughs. "I wasn't talking about you. I was talking about your character, the doctor. What's his backstory?"

"The doctor?" Vic says, then realizes. "Oh, the doctor!? Make up a backstory?" It'd be a useful exercise, he agrees. But there's a problem: The doctor is a sociopath, completely sealed off. His backstory might be difficult to uncover. Especially by himself. Would she be willing to help him? Yes? Over lunch?

Not until they're seated at the taqueria does Vic remember: He's already eaten. Weirdly enough, however, he still finds himself hungry, like his previous veggie burrito landed in someone else's stomach entirely. He orders a fish burrito this time (no cilantro). And Heather orders the beef burrito with extra guacamole, a large Diet Coke, and a plate of plantain fries.

"Now show me," he says.

"OK—who should I be?" she says through an enormous bite.

Vic glances around at the other tables. Their occupants—all set in the foreground of this wall of headshots—appear as varied as the pedestrians down at the boardwalk and yet somehow simultaneously uniform. He shrugs. "All I see are struggling actors."

"Okay," she says, and without any windup begins telling a story he could adapt. About a girl from upstate New York. Who hailed from a small town near his, a town Vic knows but doesn't remember mentioning. A girl who grew up in a small bungalow with an alcoholic stepfather. Who bought his booze with disability checks and whose sole purpose in life was to hunt. But, owing to a bum knee, the alcoholic stepfather couldn't walk through the woods and was forced to resort to other means. Such as rigging a military-grade system of headlights to his truck and driving the back roads at night with his rifle swaddled in a blanket across his lap.

"That's why I don't think I ever wanted to become a film actress," she says. "Anytime those lights shine on me, I freeze like a deer right before my stepfather shot."

"Where'd you grow up again?" Vic says. "I used to know a guy who did that."

"A few exits up the thruway from your hometown, actually."

"You're kidding."

"That's not the point. Okay—here's another example."

This story takes place in the rural Midwest. In Minnesota, a turkey farm. From an early age, the girl was tasked with overseeing the feedings of the thousand-headed flock. Twice a day, year-round, for close to a decade. Soon, she started to believe the turkeys no longer saw her. Instead, she resembled a human-shaped pile of grain. "They stalked me like tigers along the fences," she says. "The level of attention they paid me made me paranoid. Even when I was out of eyeshot, I could still feel their eyes. I can feel them watching me still, to this day. Right now, even. Always—they're with me. Thousands of beady little bird eyes. That's why, my psychologist says, I've always self-sabotaged. Fear of fame."

"One of those has to be true," Vic says.

Heather smiles. "I'm practiced. Now you try."

"Maybe we should grab a drink first," he says.

Next few days pass unmarked by any true measure of time save the gentle knocking of Vic's headboard, the pushing of its twin size back against the increasingly scuffed and dented wall. They only just met, but it seems their bodies haven't—at least to Vic, who even while pressed up against her—inside her—can't seem to get close enough.

When they can manage, they pour cheap tequila and margarita mix into Styrofoam cups filled from bags of ice they smash up with their feet against the thin carpet.

And if they manage that, they drink their margaritas down by the pool—Heather in one of Vic's T-shirts and a pair of his briefs. Vic, shirtless, in running shorts, the *Days of our Lives* script little more than an accessory where it lies unopened on his lap.

"You know you should be reading that," she says one afternoon, pointing. "You haven't even tried to imagine a backstory up."

But Vic prefers to listen to her talk—about Tucson, Memphis, New Orleans, Montreal. The places she's been, the productions she staged. The lengths her theater group went to in order to pursue their art: the homemade jars of aloe she sold, the dumpsters she dove into for food, the shacking up with random folks. The cunning of that. She can't be older than twenty-one but seems to have lived as many lives as she can describe—an impossible number of realities that make him question whether some ever happened at all.

Vic laughs. "I think you'd land any role you went out for." Clearly, she possesses a deep well of experience to draw from. The imagination, the charisma, the charm. Not to mention, an unconventional beauty that'd pop among the usual casting calls of tanned bleached-blondes.

But Heather only scoffs, shimmies off her towel, and dives into the water. Her form undulating at the bottom of the deep end before him. For too long, it seems. Glitching and writhing in the bending light. Until Vic rises from his lounge chair about to jump in after her. To wrench her sputtering from the grip of the pool. Then she surfaces, parts her curtain of raven hair—only to begin laughing at the alarmed expression he wears.

Another day passes in this fashion. Another, with the same euphoric speed of the first. Meanwhile, Vic knows he should be preparing for the taping. When only a few days ago he'd have given anything to impress the writer/producer and get roped into the murder plot, suddenly working as an actor feels like the most tedious career in the world.

Heather's slicing a lime at his desk when it happens: While inquiring yet again into the doctor's backstory, she slips, cuts herself on the blade. Then she holds the finger up for inspection. And without thinking, Vic wraps his lips around the tip and licks away the blood before pulling the finger back out of his mouth with an urgency that creates a popping sound.

He apologizes immediately. For invading her space, drinking her blood. Only a maniac would be so impulsive! "You must think I'm some freak," he says, wiping at his bloodied mouth.

At which Heather just laughs and tells him not to worry. In a way, she considers what he'd done a romantic gesture, generous even. Like a stranger offering to tie your shoe or something. She lives inside him now. Maybe he could incorporate this into the doctor's backstory somehow? And soon their laughter turns to moans again.

Next morning, a new script arrives with minor edits, watermarked with Vic's name, along with another telegram from the agent driving home the urgency of absolutely crushing this role. A solid root system for his career to flower from. "Cruise, Estevez, Lowe, *Greener*," his agent writes.

Vic slides the doctor's face back on and reads a couple of lines in front of the bathroom mirror. He sniffs and jerks back his head. But he keeps catching her reflection over his shoulder: the sheets thrown off a jutting hip, a freckled breast. A dirty foot flung sideways.

Frustrated, Vic slides the doctor's face back off, throws the script down next to a half-gone stack of headshots on the dresser, and crawls in beside her. He buries his nose in her hair and falls asleep immediately—into a dreamless void that jolts him awake upon contact, with the realization Heather hadn't followed him there. A panic that gives way to relief at the soothing warmth of her sleeping body. A cycle he's doomed to repeat, over and over, until morning.

Around ten o'clock, Heather rolls out of bed and says she's got to go. Doesn't say where, exactly. Only that she can't keep washing her sweater and underwear in his sink. She'll be back soon. Real soon. So soon that, she insists, there's no point leaving him her number, even after he hands her a Sharpie, a headshot off the dresser. Instead, she doodles a pirate's eyepatch over his arched brow, a missing tooth in his devil-may-care smile, a parrot that craps oblong blobs all over his shoulder. Before returning the headshot to the desk with the others, planting a quick kiss on his cheek, and heading out.

Does she actually have another place to stay? For the first time, Vic considers this—that she could be using him for food and shelter until her theater group heads out for parts unknown. Right now, he can't afford to wonder. He opens the script and manages to read a few lines. But his eyes keep pulling after her toward the door. Where she's only just gone, yet he keeps expecting her to return.

To distract himself, Vic showers, takes out the garbage. He pushes the bed back against the wall. Opens the script and paces. But there's no chance: The door owns his mind. Maybe she never existed, he thinks. Maybe she was part of a forgotten dream he's only now remembering.

Soon, he discovers himself searching the bed for answers: a stray black hair among the twisted sheets, or her scent on the pillow, like lemons and smoke. He shuffles through his stack of headshots with increasing desperation, unable to locate the one she'd doodled the pirate on. He pulls the bed back away from the wall to search behind it. Then the dresser. He picks up the garbage can and looks for a bottle of cheap tequila or margarita mix inside.

Terror grabs at him before he remembers: He's just taken the garbage out. But the terror remains anyway. Had he really gone down to the dumpster? The sense memory of his bare feet slapping the warm concrete teeters within him between dream and reality. *Should I go down to check?* he thinks. *And what if I find the trash bag? Should I open it? And what then? I drink margaritas by myself sometimes.*

A headache descends to wrap itself around his frontal lobe, and refuses to release. He has no choice but to lie down on the twin-size bed and close his eyes, the *Days of our Lives* script left on the bathroom counter. The front door pulling at his eyes, trying to snap open his lids to discover her standing there—

Until, eventually, there's a knock, and she's there: returned to him, a place where it feels like she's always been, and maybe had never been at all. With another bottle of cheap tequila under her arm. A bag of ice to shatter underfoot on the carpet. More laughs to laugh and moans to moan. Her raven hair like a black waterfall. The headboard knocking time against the wall.

For the next few days, Heather and Vic ride the twin size across the bedroom. When the bed becomes too lopsided, the sheets too twisted, they push it back against the wall only to begin their journey again. And when they can manage, they make their margaritas and sit poolside, where Heather regales him with stories about her life: a stint in Montreal as a street performer, playing backup trumpet in a country band in Memphis, picking blueberries for twenty cents a pint in Vermont.

When night falls, they order take-out burritos, watch bad TV as Heather doodles on Vic's remaining headshots—Vic as a cowboy, Vic a policeman, Vic a ghoulish monster with sucking voids for eyes—through which, a part of him keeps expecting, keeps hoping, for his excitement to dim. His first taping's just three days away. But Heather's attraction has a magnetism unlike any he's encountered. *Like those deer in her stepfather's headlights*, he thinks. Like his father and those foreclosed houses.

"What thruway exit did you say you grew up off of again?" he says.

Day before the taping, while Heather sleeps, Vic tries to prepare one last time. In the bathroom mirror, he slides the doctor's face on, speaks the lines. But only a facsimile looks back at hm. An empty shell of an empty shell. Tortilla chip dust.

Frustrated, he slides the doctor's face off and experiences a fleeting glimpse of the reality sure to come: the poor performance, the not being roped into the murder plot, the inevitable return to the start, the one-way ticket back into his father's endless grind—and holding the stakes in his mind, he returns to the bedroom, and slips in beside her. "You've got to go," he says.

To which Heather surprises him with her crooked smile. She throws her feet off the edge of the bed like she's only been waiting there with her eyes closed, expecting this all along. She begins pulling on her leggings, her moccasins, her oversize sweater. Then, without a word, she turns to go. As if she didn't intend to make plans to see him again.

"Wait. Never mind," he says.

"What do you mean?" he says. "This is clearly important."

"I've changed my mind."

"Don't be ridiculous."

"Promise me I'll see you again?" he says.

"You'll see me," she says with a laugh. "I'll swing by tomorrow night to celebrate your taping."

"No, I insist," he says. "Please. Stay and read some lines with me?" He shoves the script at her without waiting for an answer. He slides on the doctor's face and speaks the first line from memory: "*I've known your husband for a long time.*"

And after a few long seconds, she answers: "Funny—he's never mentioned you before."

In the scene, the doctor convinces a wife her loving husband is cheating on her. A lie meant to seduce her. They trade lines back and forth until the climax. "It says we're supposed to kiss," she says. So Vic kisses her. Or, rather, the doctor kisses her. But where the scene should've cut, the kiss continues. And they soon find themselves entwined on the bed, Heather and this doctor—as Vic watches her moan and writhe at a distance, listens to the headboard knock double-time, not so gentle now. Vic feeling the doctor's hands work upward, over her neck, to her open mouth. Her teeth biting into the heel of his palm. Red splotches blossoming all over her body—evidence of all the doctor's done to her.

And it goes on like this, much longer and further than Vic would've gone, as, behind the doctor's icy mask, he watches

Heather become someone else entirely. A stranger who makes him wonder if the depth of her desire could ever mirror his own.

"Oh, doctor!" she continues. "Harder, harder! For the love of God!"

Next morning, Vic awakes to discover another headshot—only, there are no doodles this time. Just the words *break a leg* scrawled in the background. Words he mistakes for *goodbye*.

With his head in his hands, he sits on the edge of the twin size, knowing he's being ridiculous, but unable to shake the dreadful thought that Heather's run off with another man, this sociopathic doctor. *But I am the doctor?* he thinks. But there's no time to wonder. He needs to shower, get dressed, and force the doctor's face over his own.

During the taping, the writer/director—an industry veteran—doesn't seem satisfied. Which isn't surprising. Not only does Vic keep forgetting lines, there's also something off about the kiss with the actress at the end of the scene. The writer/director keeps calling cut and waving Vic over to whisper about the obvious attractiveness of the bleached-blonde actress, the dark passions this should inspire within his character.

"Don't be shy," he says. "You two may barely know each other—but your characters are far from strangers. You've been her physician nearly her entire adult life." He wants every viewer to feel jealous of a sexual chemistry they will never have with their spouses. Can Vic do that? Can he transform himself into this doctor?

And so, Vic—not the doctor, but Vic doing an impression of this doctor—lifts the actress into the air. This radiant, blonde beauty, by all measures. And looking down, the actress holds his not-so-icy face in her hands. They stare into each other's eyes as if they are already fucking each other's brains out before she plunges her tongue into his mouth.

In the moment, the actress gives a truly convincing performance. Despite his own shortcomings, Vic believes she's actually aroused. Which arouses him, however slightly. At least enough to spur a little passion in himself until the writer/director calls cut, and he sets her down and sees the excitement he perceived drain from her face, as if it really could be faked so easily, turned on and off like that.

Afterward, when the writer/director calls him over, Vic expects to be fired. Instead, he receives a slap on the back. "Nice work out there, kid," he says.

Vic can't believe him. "You're putting me on?" he says.

"Just the opposite." In fact, the writer/director asks if he'd like to reprise the role of the doctor next week. He finds the choices Vic's making compelling, if a little unsettling, and he thinks he'd be perfect for this murder plot idea. Was Vic interested? Yes? "Don't look too thrilled," he says.

Later that night, Heather knocks at the door with a present—a bottle of cheap tequila and two burritos from the taqueria. Veggie and beef. Plantain fries. On the bed, Vic unrolls his and stares at the little green flakes mixed into the rice and beans. "I can't eat this," he says. "I hate cilantro."

"I thought you liked cilantro?" she says.

"The doctor likes cilantro."

"The doctor? What doctor?"

"You know which doctor."

"Don't be crazy," she says and starts stomping on a bag of ice for their margaritas.

"You're talking to the guy who drank your blood," he says.

She hands him a margarita. "This is different," she says. "You should be happy."

"I am happy." *Too happy*, he thinks. That's the problem: All I can think about is what I'll feel when the happiness ends. And the worst part? There's no solution. Either Heather doesn't feel the same, or she does—and in the case of the latter, they'll have no choice but to immediately get married and start having babies. Buy a house far away from Hollywood. Somewhere safe and affordable (probably the country). Where they'll proceed to raise a family, as each day their hearts threaten to burst with love. Until death takes them and they are buried in the graveyard, side by side. A life with her or without her—he doesn't know which he fears more.

So, Vic decides to conduct an experiment. During sex, he doesn't slide the doctor's face on. Instead, he follows the doctor's script while wearing his own. He strokes faster, full of dark passion, reaching for her throat and mashing at her mouth with the palm of his hand. "You like that?" he says, and her body responds accordingly, writhing and moaning. Each time he slows down to stroke more Vic-like, it's just like he feared—her passion slows to a stop, only to resume once the doctor starts up again.

After a while, he rolls off her without climax and stares at the popcorn ceiling above the twin size. The shadows hover within its texture to create thousands of tiny empty bowls.

"You sure it went okay today?" Heather says.

"They invited me back," he says.

"That's great news, right?"

"Right." But none of that matters to him anymore. Now there's only the mystery of her: who Heather prefers, where she's from, what she really enjoys. Like the doctor's backstory, he understands, there's no real knowing. That she contained too many possibilities, simultaneously giving him everything and nothing to grab on to.

And so, for the rest of the night, he spoons her, syncopating his breath with hers. Their heartbeats. He fights sleep, not wanting to lose her to the emptiness of his dreams. But the softness of her body and the lemony smoke of her hair continue to overcome him, and he drifts off, only to jolt awake again.

Sure enough, he awakes to find her gone the next morning. *Gone, gone.* Like she'd never been there at all. Even if she'd left a headshot on the dresser, explaining she'd be traveling for a few days, maybe a week, her words would've read to him like *goodbye.*

Instead of working to hone the doctor, Vic lies there—through the morning and into the afternoon. And when the phone rings that evening, his heart leaps into his throat. But it's only the writer/director calling, with what should be good news—an offer for the recurring role on *Days of our Lives*—and Vic's upset by how it isn't.

We haven't even broken up, he tells himself. If they'd been together at all.

After a few more days of sulking, Vic decides to redeclare himself to his method—to spend the rest of the day behind the doctor's face instead of his own. He steers himself toward the boardwalk, stops off at the taqueria, eats a veggie burrito with cilantro, walks on without dumping his tray. He curses at the homeless man and renews his disdain for breakdancers and small dogs. He even manages to get the walk right: the lope of a pigeon-toed wolf made jittery with coke.

Two more days pass in this fashion, three. It doesn't get easier. But the routine becomes more normal somehow. Still, he hasn't schemed up a backstory, but what does it matter? They're roping him into the murder plot now. *Vic Greener* has arrived.

He manages to tape another scene—they'd even given the doctor a name: *Reginald Mack, MD,* the script reads. A rider in Vic's contract. Health benefits. A guarantee of six months of work, three days a week now. A week and a half ago, all Vic had ever wanted.

The writer/director seems pleased with his next taping. The other recurring cast as well. Afterward, the actress Vic kissed at the last taping comes to his dressing room to congratulate him. And while she shakes his hand, he thinks he recognizes a remnant of real passion in her big blue eyes. She gives him her number, says to call her anytime, if he wants to run lines.

The work picks up. Shoots stagger every other day now. Between scenes, he memorizes obscene amounts of lines and eats veggie burritos with cilantro. Whenever he smells the rice and beans, he finds, he becomes aroused, a rigid hard-on he must fight down before standing up again. He eats so many burritos the writer/director actually makes a comment: In less than a week—just look at him—he must've gained ten pounds.

Now Vic must avoid the taqueria altogether. Even if the owner recently agreed to hang his signed headshot on the wall. If Heather had left him a number, he would've called her ten thousand times. Instead, he calls the actress, hangs up. He does this repeatedly. Late at night, sometimes—because he can't sleep, anticipating the sense of loss he experiences each time he jolts awake to his empty twin size.

Whenever there isn't a taping, Vic walks past the taqueria, sniffing at the air like a hound dog. Usually, he ends up at his ledge. Where he tries and fails to sniff and jerk back his head at more imagined cocaine gunk before giving up, proceeding to stare at the sun as his empty stomach growls. For a week, it seems, Vic sits perched there, waiting, not even attempting to mine the pedestrians for gestures anymore. Just waiting, his longing turning into superstition.

He calls the actress, hangs up again. Eventually he talks into her voicemail, trying to picture her beauty while he speaks the lines. That blonde hair, those big blue eyes. The curves of that tanned body. But it isn't long before her face fades into Heather's: those dark eyes, the upturned knuckle of her nose. The way she stood there in the sun the first time she talked to him. How she lived inside him. And the way she might return to him again, only this time crookedly smiling her forgiveness at him for the psychotic way he'd acted. The way her hand might flutter to her tongue-tied mouth, the shy smile in her eyes—a clockwork of gestures he could mine for a lifetime.

I could use that, and that. That, too, Vic thinks. *And that other thing—I can use that as well. All of it. Every last bit.* As each day he sits there, waiting, his heart leaping at the shadows cast by each passing cloud.

SUGAR BATH

Vic Greener—actor, writer, playwright, television personality, underwear model, miscellaneous, no film credits to his name— buys the foreclosure at a bank auction, on a whim, with what's left of his toothpaste commercial money. There are no other bidders.

Driving back along the pinched country highway, he thinks, *That's the universe saying thanks for agreeing to come back out to this cultureless land of pizza shops and roaring pickup trucks.* Her hometown or his, it makes no difference: Anything north of New York sprawls like a vast sort of death trap.

"I slit the sheet, the sheet I slit, and on the slitted sheet I sit."

The toothpaste commercial was over a year ago, being written off the soap a year before that, and the rest of the money Vic must beg from Mother-in-Law who never misses an opportunity to bait him—from his green breakfast smoothies to his afternoon film studies, to the way he tans, laid out in the brittle grass.

After hearing his pitch in the cramped kitchen of her bungalow, she poises pen over check and eyes him skeptically. "What about your instrument, Stanislavski?"

But today, unlike others, Vic fights himself calm, with thoughts of childhood. An apple tree, a skipped rock, the suction of a midnight movie. A tadpole netted from the murk of a pond. Through this method, he manages to produce a convincing depiction of patience. His idol, Konstantin Stanislavski (RIP), would be proud.

At least at first, anyway—because suddenly, he breaks character, discovers himself repeating a tongue twister into Mother-in-Law's reddening face. "Four furious friends fought for the phone!" he repeats. Until Mother-in-Law starts up on her own line of frustration.

The same old thing. "You're so self-involved! Irresponsible! And with a baby on the way? You should be preparing for that!"

"That's what I'm trying to do here!" Vic argues. Louder and louder. Until, finally, the whole noisy structure topples at the weak sound of Heather's voice from the guest bedroom. Where she's been laid up for the final trimester with gestational diabetes, unable to bear television light or radio sound. With nothing but a three-foot pile of what Vic assumes to be What-to-Expect-When-You're-Expecting books and the swirling ceiling fan to entertain her. More static than he's ever seen her.

"Leave him be," she says, and the small intervention proves enough—Mother-in-Law scribbles, signs.

Next morning, Vic receives the keys, drives over to the foreclosure with Heather, who insists she feels okay for a change. Could've fooled him, though. As they stare up at the foreclosure from the driveway, her pale skin resembles a wet napkin draped over organs, her cheeks a latticework of worming blue veins, her black hair helmeted with sweat around her forehead.

"This is what you're so excited about?" she says.

Vic smiles his Crest White smile. Knowing the old house isn't much to look at, Revolutionary War–old as it is, with its greening gutters and mottled slate roof. Peeling lead paint and busted-out windows with their grimacing shutters. Overgrown lawn and graveyards of flower beds choked beneath a fetid layer of decaying leaves and apple blossoms.

However, after flipping houses with his father all those years, Vic also knows these things can be fixed, an effective craft applied. That the true value is hidden in the straight rooflines, the plumbing, the sturdy foundation. "Try to see the house behind

the house," he says—a signature refrain of his father's, he realizes, before he can stop himself.

Yet the way Heather looks at him, it's as if all Mother-in-Law
says, instead of his father's words, is true: that he's just substitut-
ing one pipe dream for another. Like she couldn't imagine, even
with that brain of hers, anyone resurrecting the heap that stood
before them.

He jumps quickly to head off these thoughts. "You'll see," he
says. "A family escaping the bustle of New York will love this old
house. Three bedrooms, two baths. Two thousand square feet.
A pond, nearby woods surrounding. An apple tree. What's not
to love? Just wait. We'll be back West with our baby before
you know it. With plenty of money to burn until I can land
another role—"

Now a vulture swoops down onto the peak of the roof above,
causing his throat to hitch. Its giant wings flare wide in a six-foot
cross, then fold inward like a jackknife. A curved black feather
comes loose, drifting downward to land audibly on the front
porch like a welcome mat.

"Don't worry, doc," Heather says, reading him like she did.
"As far as my mother's concerned, you could be a panhandler and
still best any man she ever brought home—"

Vic shields his eyes, points at the purple blob of bird partially
eclipsing the sun. "You don't see it, do you?"

"See what?"

"The vulture. Staring right at you."

Heather presses her damp forehead into his shoulder. "I'm
sorry—but to tell you the truth, my vision hasn't stopped swirling since we left. I didn't want to tell you. I was afraid you'd
refuse to come. And I'd just hate to leave this place before looking inside."

So, one at a time, Vic helps her up the soggy porch stairs to the front door. Where he inserts each of the keys he received without success. Repeatedly. A dampness surfacing on Heather's taut round belly while she waits, a maple syrup smell rising off her into the air.

"Damn it . . . For fuck's sake . . . Good Christ . . ." At last Vic runs off through the waist-high yellow grass around back— dodging a chipped birdbath, startling grasshoppers into flight— toward a door with particleboard nailed into the window where the glass should've been. He tries one key, then another. He tries them again. But none of the keys fit the back door's lock either, and he must resort to shouldering open the large wooden front door.

After the lock gives, a cold blast meets them. Their noses scrunch up against the bottled must, and their eyes adjust slowly to the junk sloping from every wall, pinching the room into an epicenter of furniture: a tomb of mealy couches, identical hospital beds, a camper stove and refrigerator. A television tray full of prescription bottles.

In the doorway, Heather grips his hand with increasing strength. Then a long, hard shudder reverberates between her knuckles and her sappy hand slips away. She turns to him, wide-eyed and oddly luminous in the dark, and says, "They died here, didn't they, doc? Just look at the shape of this place. I'm afraid this is more crypt than home."

Vic starts stuffing garbage bags that same day, after returning Heather to the bungalow. To the twin bed and What-to-Expect books. To the ceiling fan and Mother-in-Law, who seems to blame him for his wife's worsened condition.

He opens blinds, spills light into the cluttered rooms, thinking how once he fixes the place up, everything will improve—Heather's health, the baby born, Mother-in-Law almost an entire continent away. Enough time to tune his instrument up for pilot season. Enough dough for childcare if Heather wanted to hunt work, too. Though he couldn't say for certain if that's what she'd want. Or what she wanted for the future at all, for that matter.

With a karate chop, he swipes prescription pill bottles into a garbage bag. Lifts a tower of medical books and dumps them in also. "Larry sent the latter a letter later," he repeats. Then he double-knots the bag, lugs the trash to the oily crag of the shoulder of the road before plunging back inside to parachute another.

In coming days, Vic disposes of furry yogurt, spoiled milk from the refrigerator. From the living room, a stiff tower of QVC magazines fused together by humidity and time. From the bathroom closet, an extensive array of spent beauty creams, wrinkle removers. Anything of value he consolidates in the living room for the estate sale.

Now there's enough room to get at the burst pipes. To fiddle with the electric, the plumbing. Peel up the moldy carpets to inspect for hardwood and estimate the damage and investment required to get a loose idea of potential profits for when the house sold. Things are better than he could've hoped. Like his father used to say, the old house has "good bones." Only now he understands the excitement with which his father said it. Meaning good septic, good well, a good opportunity. A clean bill of health, really. All it needs is a little clearing out, some paint. To replace the porch steps. Landscaping, gardening. A couple months to remedy at max.

In fact, the investment appears so sound, he decides to call his agent about lining up auditions in a few months. "Peter Piper picked a pickled peck of pickled peppers," he says into his answering machine. "It's Vic. Call me back."

The universe really seems to be realigning. Really seems ready to sync with his vision of where they desire to be: back in Hollywood with his money to burn and time to refocus on his craft. Until Vic finds the gravestones in the basement. Two of them. Jutting up like mossy teeth behind the boiler.

At first, he could've sworn there was nothing. Then his flashlight quivers, and they surface from beneath the black, packed dirt. Like two moonlit fish breaching the dark surface of a pond. One big, one small. Almost silvery. His flashlight moves across their mottled stone as he sips nosefuls of earth and fuel oil, squinting to read the names. He squints harder. But they're too rounded down. Just little bowls of dancing shadow.

The dates, however, Vic can make out fine. Mother and child, he calculates from the gothic scrawl. Aged twenty years, six days. Before a bloody death by childbirth probably. *Laid out right beneath my feet*, he thinks.

At first, he doesn't know what to do. He's never seen *this* before. Fucking gravestones!? Could this prevent him from selling the house? Should he call the cops? The town historian?

His father would know, he knows. The bastard. Would know everything and more.

And so that night, despite any misgivings, Vic discovers himself hiding in Mother-in-Law's bathroom with the landline and dialing him. Then, skipping pleasantries and blurting out everything in a low, harsh tone—about taking time off from his career. Moving back east into Mother-in-Law's bungalow. Only a few exits north up the thruway from where he grew up. Where his father still lived and worked and would no doubt do so until he died. Hoping against hope Heather couldn't hear him through the wall. And, oh, yeah, did he mention the gravestones!?

His father only laughs. The same laugh he laughed when Vic told him he wanted to act for a living. "Listen," he says. "If you come across a mysterious bone or exotic-looking beetle or even a pair of wooden teeth inscribed *George Washington*, you don't say a word. To anyone. You just heap the dirt back over and get that house sold. A police force or a county government will come and tie up all forward progress on a renovation just for something to do. They're that bored. You hear me? Think about your baby, your wife. You need to get yourself moving where you all need to go, son."

Vic doesn't mention the gravestones to Heather afterward. Instead, he lies next to her, stares at the ceiling fan while Mother-in-Law's snores radiate through the wall, and tells her about the time he fucked that aspiring actress who went on to be famous back in Hollywood. The leggy blonde who got her start on his same soap. The one he'd dated briefly after she disappeared the first time. "Remember? She was in that buddy cop movie that just came out," he says. "Anyway, she was a dead fish." Because sometimes he tells Heather stuff like that. About the wild life he'd led without her. And usually she'll listen. Get sexually aroused even, share a few of her own stories. Encounters that once upon a time might've surprised him.

Except tonight she just strokes her massive belly, thoughts clearly someplace else. "Feeling all right?" he says.

"It's just that poor couple," she says. "To think of them. Alone in that big old house. What kind of life were they living? To end up like that."

Vic stares at the ceiling fan, thinks he detects a small wobble in its rotation while debating if he should tell her that, from his experience, people generally died in this fashion. In their homes. Surrounded by the accumulation of their lives. That those were the lucky ones. If that was information that she'd find soothing. "I'm sure you can imagine," he says.

But then, when the story of the previous owners doesn't immediately begin to flow from her swollen, cracking lips, he thinks to add, "Well, what do you want to know?"

"Anything, really."

So, the next night, Vic brings her home a bowling trophy (third place). The next, a box of bank statements (money mostly spent on groceries). Then, a piece of costume jewelry—a string of plastic pearls Heather immediately drapes around her neck and pulls into her mouth and starts sucking on each bead like a lozenge.

The artifacts seem to make her feel better. Propped up on pillows, plastic pearls still in her mouth, she turns a new item in her hands each night before placing them among her growing collection, atop the What-to-Expect books that composed her nightstand.

And every night, after this ritual, she says, "Raise your right hand," and makes him promise to bring her more.

And so, Vic does—every day, it's something new: a poorly taxidermized woodpecker or a lock of ribboned hair. An ancient scrap of pornography unearthed from beneath a scratchy wool sweater. The wool sweater itself. A tattered book full of God knows what.

Recipes, Heather quickly informs him. For apple-pecan pie and flourless cake. Peach cobbler. And next to these recipes: notes, incomprehensible and scrawled in the margins. Vic can't read a word, but somehow Heather can.

"It's so much like my handwriting," she explains. *Substitute heavy cream for whole milk. Crush instead of mince. Made for Walter's forty-fourth birthday. Big success.* She might as well be making up what she reads. Her usually glassy eyes now buzz with focus.

"These all look so delicious. I'll eat them as soon as my sugars level out."

What's so exciting about this, Vic hasn't a clue. Heather having never expressed an interest in baking before. Yet now, suddenly, she's burying her nose in recipes and the foreclosure's previous owner's marginalia each night. While he stares up at the ceiling fan, trying to blink away its wobble, having to listen about milk of almonds at Christmas, homemade ice cream on the Fourth of July, he's becoming more and more convinced the ceiling fan's slight misalignment will eventually bring it crashing down.

Just as he's drifting off one night, Heather waves a photograph across his vision. A bookmark fallen from between two pages. "You awake?" she says, holding the photograph an inch from his eyes, a man blowing out a field of birthday candles in the kitchen of the old house, only cleaner and filled with light.

"For a second. I thought this was you," she says, laughing.

Vic doesn't see himself in the man. This Walter person. Not young, but not old either. Not handsome or interesting looking. Not a Crest White smile at all. Not even a little bit. He shuts his eyes, fighting himself calm, because Heather hasn't appeared this alive in months and he doesn't have the heart to kill her spirit.

"Would you look at that kitchen?" she says. "How Bohemian! How midcentury modern! Do you think that circular table's still buried in there somewhere? And what about that glassware? Is that Prohibition era? Are you sure the photo was even taken in the kitchen? I barely recognize anything from your crypt here."

* * *

Vic drags a folding table into the driveway so the pickers can see the estate sale from the road, lays out some silverware, a set of China, a box of VHS tapes with peeling labels, a circular table full of ancient coffee rings. Not much. The rest he keeps inside.

He sits on the porch steps, waiting for customers to follow the signs he'd posted on the nearby corners. He's glad to get rid of the remainder of the artifacts once and for all. So much so, he'd called his agent again that morning, repeating, "What can a clan cram in a clean clam can," into his answering machine until his tongue tied. "Shit, sorry," he said. "It's Vic. Wondering if I missed your call back." And his cheeks burn with the memory of the awkwardness of the call.

Already, a picker is approaching. And about a half hour later, the old house is mobbed. Cars line the otherwise desolate street despite the early hour. Crowds in the living room, crowds in the yard. Old folks mostly. Lots of change purses. Lots of haggling. Lots of goddamn stupid questions:

"Moving in?" they ask him. "Relative of the deceased?" Or inside the house, they try the basement door—clearly deadbolted—and ask, "Why's this locked?"

"What's down there?" they want to know, rattling the doorknob.

For the first time in weeks, Vic must employ Stanislavski's method. Must draw on his memories to feign politeness, all those paint jobs he'd sold out West. To be that salesman and convince these pickers that the scraps they bring him are worth purchasing at his costs.

This methodology comes more naturally for Heather, however. She arrives at noon with Mother-in-Law and posts up in the living room, on the old musty couch. She doesn't seem so sick at all anymore. "Seriously, I feel fine," she says while the pickers gather around her to gush and touch her belly, marvel at her, and pose questions about not only prices, but the old house itself. Many of which she surprises him by being able to answer, as if she's somehow gleaned the history of the house from the recipe book.

"If you can believe it, these flower beds used to bloom," she says. "Imagine rows and rows of lilacs, hydrangeas, foxgloves, Japanese apricots. Oh, and the vegetables, with all this black dirt—enormous!"

And what else can Vic do but stand there, wondering how in the hell she'd learned any of this? Or why she felt spinning these yarns might help sell any of this junk? *Like that ceiling fan*, he thinks, *my wife has come loose. She's off her axis. Spinning away. Just a couple of weeks ago she was on death's door, the sad state of the old house a disturbance to her, a justification of the truth contained within Mother-in-Law's doubt. Now this?*

At the end of the weekend, Vic's had enough. He drags the few remaining scraps to the curb, stakes a *FREE* sign in the grass, and for a long time just stands there, contemplating the sign's violent black marker. Then, driving back to the bungalow in his cheap pickup, he sees a sign for the thruway and contemplates turning off. In that moment, the breeze from the rolled-down window ruffles his arm-hairs, ceasing to be humid upstate New York air. Instead, it's an ocean breeze from that other world that sways palm trees, skitters sand across golden beaches peppered with tan bodies. From California. From Santa Monica. Hollywood.

Remember landing your first serious gig? he thinks. That guest spot on the soap as Dr. Reginald Mack. Remember what that felt like? Practicing your method until you basically convinced yourself he existed? How the writer/director said you crushed it. And how you became convinced that after that came something better. Something you could sink your teeth into. A place among the moment's heartthrobs, a future Mount Rushmore carved with the faces of *Cruise, Estevez, Greener, Lowe.*

Right now, it's just a matter of taking the exit. Taking 17 to 6. Jumping on 287. Then ripping that all the way back West. Going out for a pack of smokes, as they say. The old Rabbit Run. At least until the guilt swoops down to convince him everything Mother-in-Law ever said was true. That he really is self-involved. Irresponsible. Trading one pipe dream for the next. A bad husband. And a worse father, even without the baby born.

Two days overdue now. Three, now four. Vic's taped and painted the interior of the old house. Has moved outside to blast away the brittle paint with the power washer, then climb ladders with a paintbrush and bucket. Slopping the paint on with a four-inch brush, doing all he can to finish before the cold arrives and the paint won't stick. Before the baby comes. Before pilot season. Before every struggling actor floods the area, causing rental prices to spike.

"Did I mention that?" he says to Heather one night. "After this, I don't think we'll have to move back into the Oakwood. We'll be able to afford a condo. Maybe over in Van Nuys. Maybe even rent a house somewhere."

"My God—anywhere but Van Nuys," she says, still nose-deep in the recipe book. "To be honest, I'd prefer the Oakwood. I liked the pool there. I miss our friends. I miss the ocean, and the Mexican food. I miss listening to POWER 106 while sitting in smoggy LA traffic. I miss the freak scene down on the Venice Boardwalk."

Staring at the ceiling fan, her response strikes him as selfish, that she shouldn't desire more space for their child. If not an apple tree, an orange tree perhaps. A pond. More comfort than the Oakwood and its overchlorinated pool, anyway. The murmur through the cracked windows of all those struggling actors practicing lines for open calls. Something you could call a home. After obsessing about that recipe book for weeks, neglecting her What-to-Expect books in order to have a love affair with the old house. Sure, it was daunting, a large, blank canvas. But if anyone could color in a new life there for their family, it's her, if that's what she wants.

Heather's stopping by every few days now, it seems. Vic doesn't think she should be driving. But she insists the doctors say she can if she feels up to it, and she does. Mother-in-Law had just taken her to an appointment that morning.

"They say my sugars are balancing back out," she says.

Sometimes Mother-in-Law comes along with her. On these days, they walk the old house together, conspiring. "A breakfast nook would go great here," they say. "Do you really think off-white is the right color for the bathroom? What about a pastel? An earth tone?" Or: "Those wooden cabinets are so seventies—they've got to go!"

Vic hears them through the open windows where he's perched on the ladder. "I'm just trying to get this place fixed up and sold," he shouts in at them. Though they rarely respond.

Fourteen days overdue now. Fifteen, now sixteen. At least, according to the doctors. The baby still not arriving, Heather's health still somehow improving. She, still insisting the doctors say everything's all right. "A skylight would do wonders for the lighting in this room," she says.

Despite her size, she comes by daily now. To clean up the garden while Vic mows the unkempt lawn into submission. "You really don't have to do that," he says. "Take a load off. Rest. Keep doing what you have been."

Vic figures, okay, perhaps it'd be a relief to have her nearby. In case the baby comes. Or some emergency happens. Her belly has gotten so swollen that her belly button sticks out. But watching her in the garden is almost as stressful as her absence. Her bulk is really that insane to him. Strangest yet is the ease with which she bends, moves, dirt smeared across her belly like she just clawed her way out of the earth.

With a smile taut as that belly, she looks up at him. "What's wrong, doc?"

"Can't they just induce?" he says. "Is this normal? For things to take this long?"

To which, Heather—still down on her knees in the dirt—tells him that if the doctors aren't worried, why should he be? Vic's not a real doctor, right? She laughs. With gestational diabetes, it's not uncommon. "When it's too sweet in there, sometimes, the baby doesn't want to come out," she says.

Then the lawn is done. And they're staring up at the old house from the driveway. The house not so old-looking anymore. The house behind the house now fully emerged: the lush grass and hedges, the lovely walkway. The budding apple tree that Heather points out probably produced the very apples used in those recipes.

"Do you think we'll leave before they ripen?" she says.

But how's Vic supposed to know? Could take weeks, months. Might refuse to ripen until pilot season comes and goes, for all he knows. And what does she mean by asking that anyway? What's the insinuation here? Does she want to wait it out and bake pies? Is not leaving this place actually an option now? Have

Mother-in-Law's doubts led her here somehow? If she really wanted to stay so bad, he wishes she'd just ask. Make him justify his wanting to give the acting career one last go. Instead of the psyop she'd been running via the happy fiction she's made of the previous owner's life.

To head off these thoughts, Vic grabs her hand and leads her through the old house to show her. Why they couldn't make this place their home. Past the freshly painted walls and refinished cabinetry. Over the newly lacquered hardwood floors. Past the house behind the house and into the basement. Something real as life. Stair by stair, he pulls her into the subterranean dark. "Do you see?" he says, aiming the flashlight.

"See what?" she says.

"Behind the boiler. The gravestones. Now do you want to live here so bad?"

To which, Heather only laughs. "Is that what those are? What's so wild about that? People used to die at home in those days. It was probably cheaper than a church burial. Shocking—a poor farming family trying to save a buck."

"This doesn't freak you out? Having the bones of a mother and her infant in the basement of your house?"

"My house?"

"Oh, don't think I can't hear you and your mother talking!"

"Vic, honey. Please," she says. "Don't get yourself all spun up. It's just talk. What would we do with all this house, anyway? Have more children? Buy a couple dogs to sleep on the porch? Start keeping chickens? Do you picture me tending a garden for the rest of my life? No, thanks. We already have enough on our plates to mess up. Just put the house up for sale, doc. Put your mind at ease."

Yet each day after, Vic returns to tinker. Still not calling a realtor. Or his agent. He hasn't done a tongue twister since getting tongue-tied leaving that message, hasn't studied any films. A farmer's tan on both arms now. And Heather is still in the garden. Still expecting. Growing inside. The apples grow larger too. Sweetening. The soil, so rich in the yard. While Heather bends to pull the last of the weeds, and Vic stops up drafts for winter. While he baby-proofs the stairs, secures a ceiling fan in the master bedroom. Then carefully extracts the gravestones and plants them in a spot Heather's cleared out back in the garden.

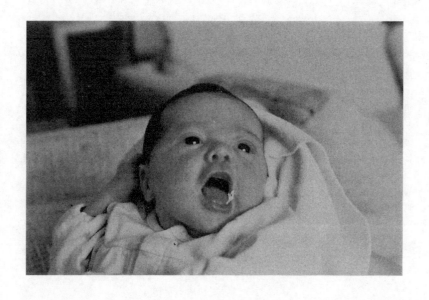

BLACK DIRT

Vic throttles the John Deere up to Rabbit, takes another swath of lawn—around the apple tree, the small pond, Heather's garden, and back again. The grass here is incessant. A second job. Ever since Heather plucked that plump tick from Junior, anything over two inches is unacceptable.

A hundred years ago, apparently, the entire town was underwater. Now the onions bubble up in the black dirt fields. And every few days, Vic must mow.

Not that he minds. In fact, he feels wonderful. Completely lobotomized. Sun-kissed and sleepy. Nostalgic, even. The breeze smacking of his childhood as a half-drunk Budweiser bottle sloshes between his knees and the vibrations from the asthmatic John Deere's engine tickles his shirtless spine.

Not that this prevents Heather from suspecting displeasure with this new role: working nine-to-five, coming home, mowing the lawn in his increasingly spattered painter whites. Clearly, she believes he's putting on some Oscar-worthy blue-collar performance. The same way he once prepared for toothpaste commercials, his brief stint as Reginald Mack, MD on *Days of our Lives*. Not that she'd articulated any of this: She didn't have to. After the way she reacted to the bull's-eye blooming at the base of Junior's skinny neck. The dangers of Lyme, a tick-borne disease he doesn't remember being a concern when he was a child.

"Stop your worry, doc. Everything is fine," was once her favorite refrain. Now what other concerns might she be hiding?

For cripes sake—he even enjoys chatting up the old folks from Valley View, that tomb of a nursing home up the road where he often threatens to send Mother-in-Law.

Here goes a trio now. Three old women shuffling up the road in the shimmering heat: the one in an electric wheelchair with short dyed-green hair, the other two with shocks of windblown white. He recognizes them from a few days ago. Thinks he does, anyway. They slow their walk by his mailbox, stop. Squint their sunken eyes against the spicy breeze and signal for him to stop, too. To chat them up again. They signal more, their frilly nightgowns flapping about what's left of them.

Yes, those are the ones from the other day, Vic decides. All of them wearing those near sweated-through nightgowns. Like they slipped past the guards on the way to breakfast. With a wave and a smile, he ignores their desperate gesturing, takes another swath of lawn under the John Deere.

The other day, perhaps he'd gotten too chummy, made the mistake of telling them—wanting to give them a thrill—about his Hollywood days. How his dreams had been deferred by his wife's surprise pregnancy. How they planned to go back West after fixing the place up but fell in love with the old house. And how he wasn't acting anymore—but busy painting houses. At least until they could buy another foreclosure to flip for some real money, anyway. "Hold on. *The* Vic Greener!?" the one in the wheelchair said. "The one and only Dr. Mack," Vic said, donning the doctor's icy mask, one he hadn't worn in years.

Then there came a reaction he didn't expect: All three old women flinched, a collective spasm of concern on their overly made-up faces. Apparently, they knew the show well. *Everyone* at the old folks home knew the show well, they then informed him. Watched it every day. At three o'clock, the halls of Valley

View echoed with the sound of Vic's voice. The mascara and blush ran down their faces now as they laughed at the thought. The black sweat dripping and speckling their thin nightgowns, splashing and sizzling on the hot asphalt at their slippered feet.

And it was all good fun until it wasn't—until their faces turned as serious as a trio of crows scowling from a far-off telephone wire. *Why did you murder Barbara? Why did you double-cross Nick? What would it have cost you to have given Detective Whitaker that safe's keycode?*

"I'll never tell," Vic said, and smiled. But his joke came out wrong. Too serious. Because then the questions kept coming, wouldn't stop: *Did you, Dr. Reginald Mack, really think you'd get away with making all that cocaine in your laboratory?*

The three old women appeared serious, waiting for him to deliver some twisted backstory only Heather could make up. Then they'd stopped asking, probing, and poking, and began telling him the consequences of what he'd done. What Dr. Mack had done. This make-believe character! The *pain* he'd caused. The seriousness of their demeanor hardening until it was impossible to find any sight of an expression beneath the wrinkled bedsheet of their aged faces, as they proceeded to tell him that his reckoning would be swift and righteous. One even pointed a long witch finger toward the house, as if to curse the life he'd been building there, the family life to which he now dedicates himself. Until, finally, he couldn't stand it: "I have to mow the lawn," he said and turned away.

So, now, today, as Vic loops back around on the John Deere and discovers the three old women still at the mailbox, he refuses to stop. Even as they gesture at him, beckoning him, trying to conjure him with their long fingers, desperately, *please*, these credulous old goats—head down, he mows.

He swigs his Budweiser dry, loops around the vast yard again. Repeatedly. And yet—

I really should take their confusion as a compliment, he thinks. That his acting had been convincing. While the other actors veered toward melodrama, he always thought his performance as Dr. Mack was more nuanced and sincere. A greasy heartthrob who hid his sociopathic tendencies behind a guise of cold professionalism. He remembers pacing the dressing room with this darkness behind his eyes, that cold block of brain. Watching playbacks, he barely recognized himself! The depraved mind inside visible. Or so he was often told—even Heather said so!

Another swath gone, with only a few more to go. One of them must've walked away (thank God)—because there's only two now. One standing, one in the electric wheelchair. Vic looks up and down the road, unable to locate the third, slightly confused because she couldn't have gone far.

The two old women are looking down at something by their feet now. Then they're looking back up and beckoning at him more, throwing their hands in the air, their long fingers casting about. Wildly. Until he begins to wonder if he should be concerned. If he needs to run inside and deadbolt the door to prevent their spells from taking hold. Then he notices the thin slip of linen between them. The slippered feet. The knocking ankles. The white hair against the deep green of the grass. He kills the engine, and the animal moan that replaces its sound is far too loud to be the lowing of the distant dairy farm. He steps off the John Deere into the partially mowed lawn and begins running, ticks springing away as he goes.

"Water," the one in the wheelchair says.

"She's collapsed!" says the other.

The third woman is screaming now. Howling, incomprehensible with pain as her dehydrated body tries and fails to right itself, the heat biting up into her from the road. But for how long now? Not too long. Minutes, at most. Yet still long enough for her to stick slightly as Vic peels her off the asphalt. For her thin skin to issue this awful delaminating sound.

What should he do with the collapsed woman hanging ragged in his arms? Her breathing rattles against him almost as hard as the mower had. He crouches down and sits her on his knee. He realigns her. Her butt, bony. Almost not there at all. Not unlike Junior, really, who's barely a toddler. His sweet, quiet boy. For a crazed moment, he fights the impulse to bounce her, hoping to elicit laughter. The nightgown has shifted slightly off her shoulder to reveal more papery skin. Almost ivory. Much like the back of his son's neck, where the bull's-eye now blossoms. She slides off again, her nightgown flapping about like a ghost. To him, with his spiking adrenaline, she seems to weigh little more than the fabric that hangs from her.

Vic hooks his arms beneath hers, drags her off the road. Into a mowed section of grass to lie there, supine. The one in the wheelchair pulling up beside him with an electronic whir. A tick clings to the old woman's face, and he brushes it off. He didn't like the sound of her breathing: too thin, too haggard. This rasping whistle he'd never heard a human make before. You didn't need to be a health professional to understand her prospects weren't good.

"Why didn't you stop for them!" Heather says. Who must've witnessed all this from the window. She's there beside him now. A glass of water in one hand. With Junior hanging in the other—an expressionless monkey, no more than twenty-five pounds—to keep away from the ticks until Vic's sufficiently mowed. The bull's-eye on his neck, so much like the old woman's reddish burns all over her body. In the mowed section of grass, like she's been mauled after only minutes in the tall grass by countless Lyme disease–infected ticks.

Vic steps back to let Heather work.

"Good question," the upright one presses. "Why didn't you?"

"We kept calling you?" the wheelchair says.

Vic doesn't know what to say. He wants to say something about fragility, about how it's all so fragile. So precious. The way our lives barrel into unknowable futures, barely giving us time to react. He loved his new life and wouldn't go back if he could. It's just that he loses the thread sometimes. Out of nowhere, the old demons rear up. He knows he should say something, but he knows it wouldn't come out right if he did.

The injured old woman manages to prop herself up. *She'll be fine*, he almost says. Then she falls back down again. Her yellow eyes roll up into her head. And her howling stops. And for some reason, they're all still all looking at him—all five of them. Pleading with their eyes for him to do something. Even Junior. Or maybe just blaming him. But for what? Regardless, under their expectant gaze, he suddenly knows what to do.

How easy the ice slides back over his face despite the heat. Shading his icy eyes with his hands, he kneels down beside the injured old woman. Picks up her thin wrist, feels her faint pulse, and imagines her stabilized in a hospital bed while placing the back of his other hand to her head. Her dentures chatter like a windup toy as the hot breeze whispers through what tick-ridden tall grass he'd yet to mow.

"Should I call someone?" Heather says. "I'm going to go call someone."

"*No*," the doctor says. "I think she's going to be all right."

"I'm going to call someone," she says.

"I said she'll be all right."

Now they all look at him like he's crazy. Then they begin looking at him like maybe he's not. In unison, his audience turns back to the injured woman in the freshly mowed grass. And for another moment, judging by their hopeful expressions, they really do believe him and expect everything to work out like he said.

EXQUISITE CORPSE

The backyard garden is a fenced-in pool of murky black Jell-O that sucks and belches up Heather's feet as she collects its monstrous and misshapen produce into wicker baskets: onions the size of bowling balls, carrots bent at right angles, apples whose fragrance draws those *fucking* deer to the fence each night to moan.

All morning, she hoists these loaded baskets into the bed of Vic's pickup for the farmer's market, a new endeavor in which her husband has all but refused any help because "Sundays are for taming the lawn."

Returning for a final basket, Heather hears a muttering from behind the blackberry bramble. Near the half-sunk gravestones that Vic, in all his wisdom, wedged in the far corner of her garden. She removes a pair of gloves hung on a nail for such occasions. (Too many mornings, she'd come out to weed only to discover a dead gopher or rabbit drowned in the dirt.) But today it's only Junior, her four-year-old son. Berry-stained, sunk to his kneecaps.

At first, he doesn't notice her. Silently, he appears to sink toward his death without struggle. Resigned—like he wanted to pass into the soil, a little suicidal seed. His small hand moving between mouth and bramble as between mouthfuls, he proceeds to mutter the nonsense language that still dredges her worry. Even after the specialists confirmed he was within a normal developmental range. Not mute, not deaf. No neurological deficiencies because of his bout with Lyme. That this silence has nothing to do with the diet of bizarre produce he'd been eating since he could swallow a solid bite.

If none of these, however, then what? The list of possible causes stretched on and on.

Junior's murmurs fall silent. He lifts his arms, clasps his fingers around her neck as she strains to free him, the black dirt gurgling with every inch of him it gives her—

A pair of shins.

Ankles.

With a final belch, the toes.

Yet, where the tension should've released, the tension remains. A root? A stone? An undead hand, trying to steal her baby!? Dear God—what an imagination she has. Only, the black dirt really doesn't want to release him, keeps trying to pull him down. Until, suddenly, Junior comes free with a popping sound.

Heather hugs him, cooing softly. As if he were crying, like she imagines another little boy might, instead of this affectless mask that reminds her of Vic's icy doctor. Even in the face of drowning— as if he saw all of what she and Vic had to offer and didn't feel too passionate about sticking around.

Then something bumps against the leg of her blue jeans—a necklace, Heather realizes, setting Junior down. It's dirt-caked and rusted. How would such a thing even get down there, she wonders, turning the pendant in her hand.

Sure, the house is old (the date on the gravestone over in the corner reads *1801*). But she sees no reason that a necklace such as this should be bubbling up in any backyard. Unless the previous owners had lost the necklace. Or worse: It'd slipped off another body that'd been buried nearly two centuries ago, from a wooden coffin now shipwrecked with rot.

If there were two graves in the basement, why not graves out here in the yard? Ridiculous, she knows. But when did that ever stop life?

A farmer with a tombstone-shaped head sells small containers of artisan goat cheese at the booth next over. And at ten dollars apiece! The shoppers slip them into canvas bags all morning long. Meanwhile, Heather sells nothing.

Perhaps Vic had been right about the farmer's market. Perhaps, for them, the answer was and always would be finding the next foreclosed house. Selling vegetables, much like painting houses, he argued, wasn't going to amass them any real wealth. Wouldn't take them where they wanted to go.

"And where's that, exactly?" she said.

"Paris? Morocco? Cancun?" he said. In the moment, she'd laughed at him—but that didn't mean he was wrong.

Much like last week, the shoppers tend to gawk instead of buy. To pump the freakish produce like weights, take a photo, move on. But to deny the wonder of the vegetables that grew in this yard: This would also be difficult. "I'm about to rebrand as an all-natural gym," Heather tells the tombstone-headed farmer. "Or start a vegan freak show."

But he's too busy accepting ten-dollar bills to chuckle. His buck-toothed smile says it all: *these idiot yuppies*.

A few booths over, a woman in a white dress and a crown of roots tunes a guitar on a stool, readying to sing a song. "Sibilance," she repeats into the microphone. "Sibilance . . ." Until, finally, old tombstone-head turns to Heather—his head going from thin to broad, and says, "What was that you said?"

"Never mind," Heather says.

Yet he keeps staring at her. As if x-raying through her flannel shirt to photograph her naked body. This perverted gnome! Or so she thinks until she remembers the necklace: sliding it on. The emerald or jewel pressing coldly against her chest, staining her collar with earthy trails of degrading metals, the bits of dirt caught in her jeans' waistband. She pulls the chain taut against the back of her neck so he can get a better gander. "Exquisite," he says. "Where did you find it?"

"At some estate sale. Out in the black dirt."

"Where, exactly?"

"I don't remember." Heather doesn't know why she lies. Or why she slips the rusty necklace inside her shirt and busies herself rearranging enormous heads of cauliflower no one will buy. But old tombstone-head just keeps staring. "I'll give you twenty dollars for it," he says, unrelentingly.

"For what?"

"That necklace."

"This worthless thing?"

"Fifty."

In her palm, Heather reevaluates the necklace. What had she missed? Despite having hosed most of the dirt off, the pendant isn't any more impressive, any more revealing. Just clearly brittle, its lines less defined. The pendant itself cracked, about to fall away at any moment from the spidery fingers that held the smoky quartz–looking stone at its center. "It's not gold or silver far as I can tell. No diamonds," she says.

"Seventy-five, highest offer."

"Is there some kind of historical value you're not mentioning here?"

Now another shopper—a young, pregnant woman—approaches him, holding eight containers of goat cheese for purchase. "Is this cheese pasteurized?" She stands there patiently while the tombstone-headed farmer begins peeling off tens from the wad he unsheathed from his dirty jeans pocket. "A clean eighty then," he says, ignoring the pregnant woman.

"No way," Heather says.

"One hundred?"

"I think I'll give it as a Mother's Day present."

"Two hundred."

"What's going on here, exactly?"

And for another moment, his eyes remain dark, squinting. Like how Junior's squinted back in the garden. Like Vic's doctor. Then he blinks, turns away. The spell broken—his broad head going thin again as he says, "Nope, it's raw and super fresh," and accepts the pregnant woman's money. And someone lifts one of Heather's eggplants like a barbell again. A flashbulb explodes as, in the distance, a guitar strums and an angelic voice sings a Nirvana cover. Another person hoots at her monstrous vegetables with laughter.

At dinner that night, Vic can't believe she didn't sell the necklace. Her vegetables certainly weren't raking in the money. And it wasn't gold or silver as far as he could tell. Didn't have any diamonds or rare-looking stones. "And the farmer wanted how much?"

"I already told you."

"And you found it where?"

"I told you that, too."

"It just doesn't add up," he says, looking from her to Junior. On the table, a great roasted cauliflower steams like a boiled brain. Through the fog of which, Junior pokes at a cross section, chews. He doesn't stare at his plate, but straight through it.

"How'd your day with Daddy go?" Heather asks him to change the subject.

But Junior just keeps chewing without answer, staring into the cauliflower's sloughing folds. A nervousness to him, as if beaten into this silence. But by whom or what? Heather can't imagine. His sense of love and security are all that matter to her, to them. If the specialists haven't missed anything, if the silence truly doesn't generate from within, whose fault is this? "Junior?" she says. "Did you help Daddy mow the lawn today?"

Still, silence pervades.

And pervades.

Today it's Vic's turn. Moments like these, usually, someone will step in. To diffuse Junior's glaring vacancy enough to allow the moment to move on again. By playing a version of their old game of making up stories, creating a backstory for his distraction. Perhaps, this afternoon he'd say something like, "He sure did. Sat on my lap the entire time. He even took the wheel and drove, didn't you, son?" Then with a higher pitch to his voice— think a stuttering baby meets Mickey Mouse—he'd respond, "I sure did, Da-da-daddio. I turned that John Deere all the way up to ra-ra-rabbit and mowed the heck out of that la-la-lawn." Yet, tonight, Vic just keeps chewing his cauliflower and staring at the necklace with the same frozen squint as old tombstone-head from the farmer's market.

"Let me see that thing again, will ya?" he says, finally.

Now Heather pulls the chain taut against the back of her neck again, holds out the rusted pendant.

"No," he says. "I mean, can I hold it? Let me hold it," he says.

Heather can't conjure any reason why he shouldn't. Why the comfort they'd enjoyed these past few months had suddenly vanished. So, after another moment of consideration, she hands him the necklace. And he stares into it, at his palm.

"Maybe there's historical value," he says after a while.

"That's what I thought. But to discern that at a glance? I didn't tell him anything."

"You sure you didn't?"

"Nope."

"Okay," he says. "Maybe I'll swing by the jeweler for an appraisal tomorrow, then?"

"All right," she says.

"All right," he says.

"All right, fine," she says.

"Fine, then," he says. And as his hand closes around the necklace and disappears into his pocket, Heather wants to throttle him. To dig her nails into his flesh. She has no idea why. Only knows that she doesn't want to wait until tomorrow to have the necklace back.

She looks at Junior, wondering if he even notices when they fight like this—if their moments of tension he's witnessed, however small, have prevented him the opportunity of expression—then toward the window where night's fallen. The dark glass throws their dull reflection back at her: a superimposition of a family hovering within the square of blackness. This shape they've formed. Slightly distorted by the old glass. Not theirs but a different one, with no sad looks upon their faces. As if long ago, the house itself had sunk into the black dirt of the garden and trapped them there to wait until they were yanked up again. Reborn: safe, secure, and perfect. Their intentions glued together by an eternity of black muck—

A crazy thought.

*　*　*

Next morning, after Vic drives off for work, Heather enters the garden in search of answers, a short-handed shovel in hand, a rubber mallet. The black dirt fights for possession of her feet as she makes her way along the rows, to the blackberry bramble, with Junior inside, watching TV—an activity which he seemed content to do for endless hours.

All morning, she drives the shovel into the black dirt, pounds it deeper with the rubber mallet, works the shovel back up, hoping its edge will hook something—anything; some sign of what else is down there; an answer—while simultaneously knowing how dumb this sounds.

After a while, she grows desperate, begins calling for her son. Until, eventually, she can hear the black dirt sucking at his feet as he makes his way to the back corner of the garden. "Take your shoes off and eat some blackberries," she says.

His hand moves to his mouth without any real expression. Back and forth—as his toes sink, then his ankles. And his shins disappear, too, without any sign of stopping, so she strains to pull him out.

For the rest of the morning, Heather repeats this. She can't help it, allowing her son to sink a little deeper each time. His knees, his stomach. But each time she comes up empty. No jewelry. No clues for this wonder, no signs.

Vic enters the kitchen that night with his usual routine: He tousles Junior's hair, pours himself a drink. Sits at the table to catch them up on his workday of painting this intricate farmhouse. "A Painted Lady," he says it's called. For two Canadians who may be twins or lovers. Real tabloid stuff that'd usually interest her. Except tonight.

On the table, another cauliflower steams alongside bent carrots.

"Get to the part about the necklace?" she says, finally.

"Ah, the necklace . . ." Her words seem to have set off a desperate spasm in him. He pats the sides and rear pockets of his painter's whites. The cargo pockets. The sides and rear again, before lifting his Carhartt vest off the back of his chair, rifling through those pockets as well. He curses softly, then louder. Then bolting upright, his finger fishing inside the collar of his T-shirt.

Then, with a yank, finally, ah, yes: the necklace.

"Thank God," she says.

"The appraiser had me going," he says. "Must've spent forty-five minutes peering through that eyeglass. But, yeah, you should've sold it to the farmer when you had the chance."

"Worthless then."

"Worthless." Vic tucks the necklace back under his paint-flecked T-shirt and resumes shoveling the soft cauliflower into his mouth. Like he'd thought he'd keep it. As if he could decide. And when Heather raises her eyebrows—a gesture she feels should've clearly expressed her desire for him to hand the necklace back—he just keeps eating. Oblivious as his son.

"Can I see the necklace please?" The enunciation of the words is so perfect, so clean, that she shivers. An adult voice, honed over years. She looks around the kitchen, thinking of the previous owner's ghosts before she thinks of her son. But no one else is here. Of course it's her son who'd spoke them.

But had he really? Junior pokes at his food, chewing in silence. They look at him, back at each other. "You heard that, right?" Vic says. "I heard that," Heather says.

Is that how my son's voice sounds? she thinks. Of course, he *can* talk—but with such perfect diction? She feels awful for having neglected to show him the necklace sooner, for keeping it hidden beneath her flannel.

Vic must feel similar because next thing he's wresting the necklace from beneath his collar, handing it to him with quivering fingers. "Isn't it pretty, son?"

"It's full of history," Heather says.

"*How did it get into the garden?*" Junior says, pitch perfect.

Heather and Vic exchange another glance: a transmission of the shipwrecked coffin, the shrunken body. As if the story of the house's history could have only been revealed with Junior's question.

"How do you think it got down there?" Heather says.

Junior doesn't answer, stares into his palm, wearing that same expressionless gaze. Like the person who'd surfaced just moments earlier had already returned to the black hole from which he'd just emerged. The possibility of reappearance hovers in the room, makes them desperate to hear his voice upon them again, like some highly addictive drug.

"Someone must've buried it," Vic says, answering for Junior now.

"Like treasure," Heather says, joining in.

"Two hundred years ago they didn't have many banks!"

"They buried things."

"Did you know that, Junior?"

"Son?" Despite their efforts, his speechlessness remains a reinstated blackness that muffles their words, forces them silent as Junior continues staring at the necklace. At its rusted chain. Its brittle pendant and smoky stone. His attention, so much like that of the tombstone-headed farmer's as he'd carefully scrutinized its intricacies earlier that day.

"You're lying," Junior says, finally.

"We're lying?"

"We'd never."

Junior's eyes narrow. "I know how they bury dead bodies. I know our house is old and people lived here before us. Multiple generations. I know they died because they don't live here now. I do go to preschool, you know."

"That's right," Vic says.

"Brilliant," Heather says, laughing and crying. "My smart boy."

"The daughter who died had a big, round belly," he continues. "She was pregnant with a farmer's baby son. I know a lot of other things, too," he says.

"A storyteller," Heather says.

"Like his mother." Vic says, his eyes welling. "What else do you know?"

"I know her husband was an ugly fox. And I know her father traded her dowry for a sack of onions. He often drank instead of worked. I know he had three fingers blown off in the war—"

"What war?"

"Revolutionary," he says, speaking words as if reading them from his palm now.

Then, silence again: Junior, receding below the surface of himself. Staring into his palm still, the necklace. Transfixed. With each subsequent moment, the strange digression becomes stranger, more dreamlike, as if it hadn't happened at all.

"And what happened to the last of them?" Heather asks.

Yet, still, Junior says nothing. Deaf, mute again. Their motionless and silent son.

"A pregnant woman died. She was buried in the garden—"

It's not Junior who speaks this time, Heather realizes. But Vic's voice, Junior's proxy. The stuttering baby/Mickey Mouse again. How she's used to hearing him. The Junior she knows.

Not this small stranger in a high-chair with a head that barely clears the table. As he stares at the necklace with him. Both sporting the same expressionless face. Like something else is speaking through them. Then Junior says, "Between the three oak trees out in the yard . . ."

Then Vic: "The husband went mad with grief . . ."

The game is becoming obvious, an old improv game, and Heather jumps in now: "They planned to have ten children . . ."

"The husband hanged himself . . ." Junior continues.

"In the garden . . ."

"To be with her . . ."

"In the garden . . ."

"Where, to this day . . ."

"They still knit . . ."

"The roots . . ."

"We . . ."

"Eat . . ."

"Into . . ."

"Animals . . ."

"For their . . ."

"One and only . . ."

"Beloved child . . ."

The cauliflower grows limp as the clock stops ticking on the wall. And the night grows impossibly darker. Stranger yet—the joy that now fills the room. This culmination of all of it, everything. So joyous. The goal, simple: to prolong the dream until it becomes reality. Around and around the table, their game continues. On and on and on.

THROUGH THE WALL

It's weird at first: the tenants through the wall, inhabiting what used to be one-half of their home. Their clanging pots and toilet flushes, creaking footsteps. The second truck in the driveway beside Vic's at night and the ache in Heather's breast whenever their newborn cries.

The tenants make it easier, however. This seven-foot-tall garbageman and mousy stay-at-home mom. The way they fill the extra square footage of their house that had otherwise gone unutilized: with their muffled laughter and conversations, the shoes lined up neatly on the welcome mat by the second entrance in the side yard. The wind chimes hung high up in the oak tree. The rent stuffed in a dirty envelope and paid on time—

In this way, after a few short months, the sound of their living reduces to a common sound. Like the boiler rumbling in the basement or the ever-shifting bones of the old house. The coyotes that yap off in the woods at night.

The supplemental income gives them some room to breathe. The bulk of their savings tied up, as it is, in their first flip house. So much so, Heather believes they can afford a vacation. What would be their first. Vic laughs at the prospect, thinking she's making up stories again. "No, really, doc," she says, looking over the numbers in a notebook. They owe it to themselves, after the year they've had. But the discussion goes no further that night.

And for a while, their lives continue as usual: Heather with Junior, savoring her last year with him before kindergarten. Working in the garden, trying to sell what they can't eat themselves at the farmer's market. Vic renovating the foreclosure they hope to convert into another rental, this disheveled colonial they purchased at auction for a prayer. Until one night, after looking over the numbers again, Heather says, "If we do it on a budget, I really think we can swing it."

"Swing what?" Vic says.

"A vacation."

"Hilarious—next thing you're going to suggest we fly back West for pilot season," he says. Heather's serious, though. Has already purchased the tickets, in fact. Made arrangements with her mother to have Junior stay with her at the bungalow and more than that: They're all set to spend an all-inclusive vacation in Puerto Vallarta, if Vic wants. The vacation they'd never had. The first time they'd be alone overnight in how many years.

"Wait—you're not fucking with me, then?" he says.

"Would you be mad at me if I wasn't?"

"Of course not. I'd be thrilled. But there's just one thing—" And he throws off his covers and stands before her on the hardwood floor with his chest puffed out, his shoulders back, his fists at his waist like a superhero. "You may no longer refer to me as this *Doc* character," he says with all the gravel in his throat that he can muster. "Consider the good doctor's medical license hereby revoked for malpractice. And the cops are growing suspicious about what he's been cooking up in his lab. Now he's suspected to be on the lam in upstate New York with a new identity via his cocaine connects down in Miami. And he isn't coming back—yes, *Dr. Mack* shall henceforth be known, and only respond to, the *American Berserker*!"

A few days pass, then a week—before Heather notices the garbageman's truck in the driveway. How it stays there for days, unmoved. While Vic's off at work, she thinks she hears the garbageman with the stay-at-home mom, his hulking presence creaking beams, the basso profundo of his voice shaking the walls. Like it always had, only different now, at these odd hours that he used to be at work.

"I know it's silly," she tells Vic in bed that night. "But it's beginning to concern me. I think he's been fired from his job."

To which, Vic responds, "It *is* silly." The garbageman only concerns her because he's a seven-foot-tall garbageman—the slasher from the yet-to-be-made horror film, *The Seven-Foot-Tall Garbageman Massacre*. His otherworldly height is obscuring her perception of his humanity, that's all. If he was the five-foot-tall garbageman, she wouldn't feel this way. No one would be interested in seeing a *The Five-Foot-Tall Garbageman Massacre*, right?

The garbageman's probably just been coming home for lunch, anyway, he continues, trying to save some money. They just had a baby, right? And a freakishly big one at that. "They're just starting out, Heather. Not unlike us." he says. "Don't worry about them."

"I didn't say I was worried," she says.

But then the interaction in the garden happens—Heather's weeding when the garbageman emerges from his side entrance and lingers to talk. He'd smelled whatever it was she'd been cooking that morning and was wondering if she'd give him the recipe. And when Vic comes home, she's seriously freaked out. She shows him the deep impressions the garbageman's feet left in the black dirt of the garden, imitating the way his teeth gnashed up ice cubes of the drink he held in his enormous hand. The way the tops and bottoms of his eyeballs showed while he tried to guess what she'd been cooking:

"Pears," he said, snapping his fingers. "No, apples. Red Deliciouses? Never mind. Granny Smith, then? For apple strudel?" he said. "No, no, no. Scones? A tart of some kind? Don't tell me. I can tell I'm getting close by that look in your eye. Praline-glazed strawberry-rhubarb pie?"

Then his voice shifted to a whisper: Was strudel the same thing as a turnover? And how exactly did a cake differ from a pie? The crust? Had she ever seen a cake with a crust before? But before she could answer, he continued guessing as if not expecting one as he followed her inside, only to loom there in the kitchen while she copied down the instructions from the previous owner's recipe book for the simple apple pie that sat cooling on the countertop.

Ever since, she says, she's been tiptoeing around the house so he won't think she's home.

"Wait . . ." Vic says. "You let him inside?"

Heather points at the slash of grease his hair left on the ceiling. "I didn't exactly invite him," she says.

"What do you want to do?" Vic says, a little concerned now. "Kick them out?"

No, Heather doesn't want to do that. Heather can't distract their family from the care of their newborn by upending their lives. Like he said, they're just starting out. And anyway: She isn't afraid for her well-being. Not exactly. Her privacy, yes. But she doesn't think he'll hurt anyone. In the moment, she just felt this knee-jerk instinct to protect herself, protect Junior—a response she probably wouldn't have felt, as he said, if he was five feet tall.

"I just think they need a little more time," she says, speaking low, like the garbageman might be listening. "There's only a couple more weeks until our vacation. I'm sure things will look very different by then."

"I'm sure," Vic says, shaking his head: "Your imagination has always been a wild one."

* * *

Then the first of the month passes. "They've probably just forgotten," Vic says. But the envelope doesn't show up in the mailbox on the second, either. Or the third. Or fourth. Or the fifth after that. And each day they come closer to their vacation, Vic and Heather listen a little more closely through the wall. To the toilet and pots and footsteps, the garbageman's talking. The sounds, no different than before but made precarious by their discomfort.

The day before vacation, they agree: Vic has no choice but to go over there. To play the part of Evil Landlord. So, first thing, he stands at the side entrance, knocking. And when no one answers, he attempts to peek through the gaps in the blinds. Finding the apartment dark, he knocks harder. Keeps knocking, swearing to himself that he just heard them eating breakfast. But there's only silence—save the wind chimes—despite the shoes on the mat.

He's about to leave when the stay-at-home mom finally answers, struggling to cradle a hulking newborn in her rail-thin arms. "I'm sorry," she says, trying to blink away the weariness in her eyes. "We fell asleep in front of the TV. Please come inside."

And as Vic steps into the darkened apartment, she begins to inform him about a clogged drain. In the bathroom. Apparently, the fiberglass bathtub he put in on the cheap refuses to empty, the pipes of the house, so ripe with ancient grime. The garbageman hasn't a chance to snake it clean, working as hard as he's been to keep them in diapers and the extra formula she needed to satisfy the newborn's ravenous hunger. Would Vic look at the drain while she fetches the rent money?

"Of course." Vic feels no relief at these assurances. He'd just heard the garbageman creaking about the apartment moments ago. Or had he? The garbageman loomed so large these past few days, his presence never truly dissipated. Had he passed the garbageman's truck on the way over? He can't remember. And even if he had, there's always the chance he'd caught a ride—because where would a person like that hide?

With a polite smile, Vic enters the small bathroom and is immediately confused by what he discovers: the plastic bath tub is empty. His breath catches when he turns to find her, standing in the doorway with her newborn, offering no explanation for the discrepancy. Just pinning him there. Then she starts talking: about the seven-foot-tall garbageman, the recent developments in the life they shared. Her hands trembling beneath the massive infant, clenching no dirty envelope, as far as he can see. She breathes heavy with exhaustion as she goes on about how the garbageman had been laid off weeks ago after a relapse. How he was prescribed something after a minor injury at work. An upper. By an idiotic doctor. To help him focus to study for a recertification he needed to operate the heavy machine. And how it wasn't his fault—the way it caused him to relapse, she explains, tearing up. He's a good man, a hard worker until this little slip up. Until her story has taken command of the room, every bit as hulking as her husband's presence. "He'll come back," she tells him. "He always does," she says.

Then the stay-at-home mom falls silent, allowing her story to take hold. The infant rooting at her breast like a giant piglet, as if to drive her helplessness home. Like she might satisfy him with the gallons of milk no human her size could produce.

Therefore, it takes Vic a few seconds to realize what's happening, the question she's posing with her silence. And he thinks about his answer for a moment. Thinks longer than any true

American Berserker should—because then the actor in him takes over and begins to empathize, if only for a moment, placing himself inside her life.

He shouldn't have—because just then, something like hope twinkles in her welled-up eyes. A slow upturning of the corners of her mouth, which makes what he must explain next that much harder: that he, that *they*, need the money. That her family's personal issues aren't his concerns. He has a family, too, she needs to remember. And in their own way, Vic's family is struggling as well. If she can't pay the rent without the garbageman, there will be no slack cut. No month forgiven. And if she has no way of earning the money herself, he thinks it'd be best that she should vacate the premises by the end of the month. To be gone by the time they returned from their vacation, if possible.

"I know how this looks. It's not personal. It's just business," he says.

Next morning, Vic packs his luggage: board shorts, flip-flops. A Xanax wrapped in a tissue for the flight. Another Xanax with breakfast to stanch the worry Heather instilled last night: "You could have waited until we got back," she said after he'd come home and told her what he'd done. "I thought it'd be better to get things moving," he said. "I thought this was what you'd have wanted?"

"What I wanted? What if he comes back?" she said.

"To do what?" he said, and she started listing offenses:

Concrete down the toilet.

Rat poison sprinkled down the well.

Holes punched in the Sheetrock.

Copper wires ripped from the wall.

Grand larceny, arson, violence, murder. Need she go on? To which Vic said, no, she needn't. He understood now. He'd royally fucked up. He thought he'd been doing right by his family and instead did wrong. "Trust me," he says. "No one hates me more than me right now."

On the plane now, Vic drinks a double scotch. Unwrinkles a second Xanax, breaks off half for Heather, who's already busy unscrewing a second plastic bottle of white wine. They sit there in the chilly artificial air of business class, not speaking—because they agreed not to discuss the tenants anymore, but can't think of anything else to talk about.

They don't hold hands or watch the movie as, out the window, the clouds morph into a low, flat, gray wall. The other travelers are festive, talkative, getting a jump start on the fun— but not them: Heather doesn't even finish the Sudoku puzzle in the back of the in-flight magazine before the plane touches down.

Stepping into the blinding x-ray light outside the small airport, a line of taxi drivers jockey for their fare like paparazzi at a red-carpet movie premiere. Heather waves down the most desperate-looking: a small man with a scar on his face and a white, button-up, polyester dress shirt three sizes too large. He drives them through small towns so far gone Vic wouldn't even know where to start renovations—the thin, dilapidated walls, crooked roofs of corrugated steel, tarp-covered roofs. Barbed-wire fences, collarless dogs, and gutted cars.

The taxi driver points at a clump of them and tells them that's where he lives, with his wife and small child. Too many people to fit, he says in broken English. "But we manage," he says. "We work hard." Before offering and selling them two beers from a

cooler that's been seat-belted into the passenger seat for an inordinate price. They sip them quietly, watching a Mexico they'd
never visit whiz by.

Once safely inside the resort's gates, Heather pays the driver,
tipping him a substantial sum. Meanwhile, a child not much
larger than the garbageman's infant son scurries out of the shade
of a palm tree and into the dry heat to fight the luggage from
Vic's hands. Struggling to balance the largest suitcase on his
head, the child then leads them to the front desk in the open-
aired lobby, where a woman with a roan tooth gives them wrist-
bands and shots of tequila, which they accept readily. "Everything's
included," she says. "Except for the Jet Skis. Those are an
upcharge."

As the bag boy leads them to their room, he kicks sun-drunk
iguanas out of the way. At the door, he extends his child's palm
for their key card and opens their suite for them. Then he drops
the luggage on the king-size bed and stands there, waiting for Vic
to tip him.

He does. Generously—a twenty from the dirty envelope that
contains what's left of the garbageman's last month's rent. The AC
unit mutters on the wall, fluttering a pair of long drapes knitted
with sunsets. But the bag boy remains, as if the tip isn't sufficient.
Lingers there on the orange shag carpet of the room, rocking on
his heels, looking at his scuffed tennis shoes. Finally, he produces
a small baggie—of marijuana—from his pocket, whispering a
modest price for them to consider. Which Vic pays out of pity as
Heather disrobes from her bikini in the background, thinking the
bag boy already gone. Oblivious and pale, she stands there, naked
before his small, dark eyes.

* * *

Once in the pool, they wade toward the bar—the green, overchlorinated water shimmering around them—to order margaritas. Perched there on concrete seats submerged in the water beneath the cabana, Heather talks a little: about the resort, the weather. She glances around at the other vacationers, trying and failing to make a guessing game of what each does for a living—because they're all so clearly landlords.

They order a second round from the handsome Mexican tending bar. They're talking a little more now: about how when they first met, they used to crush bags of ice against the floor of his apartment for margaritas. Now look. How lime-y! How frothy! How smooth! Who in their right minds would have predicted their lives ending up this way? "Not me!" Heather says.

And then a third drink—while they watch a fleet of Jet Skiers crosshatch the horizon, the blender's chortles rising above the sounds of the mariachi band that plays through speakers hidden somewhere behind the bar.

Neither has drank much since having Junior or put anything in their stomach that day besides Xanax, and they have become drunk rather quickly. When Vic reaches into his pocket to tip the handsome waiter, the small baggie of marijuana falls into the water, floating off on the currents of the large pool. He waves at it, laughing.

"A skunk sat on a stump," he says. "And thunk the stump stunk—ah, fuck."

"We should probably eat some dinner," Heather says, laughing along. "Before you truly do get cuffed for drug trafficking, good doctor."

"That's the *American Berserker*!" Vic corrects, so loud that many at the bar look in his direction.

They enter the open-air restaurant holding hands. Standing close, they shuffle along the sneeze-guard of the buffet, piling plates sky-high with tamales and spaghetti, dinner rolls. Sushi stuffed with cream cheese. Whatever they can fit. An international spread, if there ever was one.

While they eat, a waiter darts in and out, offering more tequila. More numbing fun. Somehow the same handsome Mexican who'd been tending bar. When Vic accepts a shot, the bartender/ waiter leans his head back, drapes a napkin over his eyes, pours some down his throat from a long, unmarked bottle with a silver spout before taking Vic's head in his hands and rocking it back and forth. "Boom, boom, boom," the bartender/waiter says, until Heather's laughing hysterically. "Boom, boom, boom."

"Again, again," she says, wanting to take a picture with the disposable she'd forgotten purchasing at the airport. "Say, 'Greedy, greedy gringo!'" she says.

"*Greedy, greedy gringo!*" Vic says along with the bartender/ waiter.

Afterward, it's sunset. Late Jet Skiers skip across the purpling water. In the distance, samba music echoes. A small band shell stands off near the beach. Where, closer now, they can see that people appear to be dancing. The trail is clear of iguanas as Heather drags Vic toward the music.

On the dance floor, awkward couples in floral prints sway, and they join them. A tall, handsome man moves between them to encourage better form. The same man from the restaurant and the bar, Vic realizes. When the bartender/waiter/ dance instructor finally works his way to them, he pushes their crotches together, and says nothing. Leaves them like that.

Swaying—back and forth, back and forth, a heat rising up between them, a delicious dampness seeping up into the hands they've placed upon each other as the first of the stars emerge overhead and the Jet Skiers continue to skip across the darkening ocean. The earth rotating over the horizon. Heather's cheek on Vic's shoulder, the lemony perfume of her hair filling his nose.

PRESSURE TREATED

The garbageman can cut a line along an eight-foot ceiling without a ladder. The garbageman can churn concrete like butter, demo walls by bursting them with a lowered shoulder. Not to mention, he wasn't lying when he told Vic he's skilled with his hands: He's completely capable of the fine finishing work that Vic would've had to hire out for.

"And all this for pennies!" he tells Heather one night in their queen-size bed. "I've heard you can work three times as fast with two people, but this is ridiculous."

Tonight, it's the same story, like every night these past few weeks: Vic wants Heather to sign off on a home equity loan on their house. His eye, already on their next project, this partially burned-down Cape Cod on which he wants to bet everything they have. That way, he explains, they could keep the garbageman working for them full time and prevent him from returning to his old job hauling asbestos and biosolids at the waste company.

"Of course the arrangement wouldn't be forever," he says. "Just for a little while. Just until everyone finds their footing and we start moving where we need to go."

"And where's that, exactly?" says Heather.

That's simple, Vic explains: on to the next foreclosure, and then the foreclosure after that. And so on—one after another, after the next, renting or selling them until they amassed a fortune large enough that they could do whatever they ever wanted. Buy a king-size bed, for example? Some sheets with a high thread count? They could hire someone to mow their lawn. Shit—they could put a pool in the backyard and Junior could spend his summers splashing around while they sipped margaritas in lounge chairs, talking dirty to each other under their breaths.

"A bigger bed?" Heather says. "You trying to get away from me or something?"

"Never in a million years," Vic says. But they should consider the long-term: There'd be Junior's college tuition. Or, better yet, the financing of Junior's first flip house. Not to mention, he's bound to get married and will need help with a wedding and honeymoon. Or, if not that, then, surely, something else. And, of course, they'd want to travel. And they'd need enough money to go wherever, whenever, they wanted, without a second thought. Maybe buy a second home on the West Coast (maybe Malibu or Laguna Beach) where they'd divide their time: seeing old friends, watching sunsets? Maybe they'd even produce one of the old scripts he'd written?

"You know I'm kidding about that last part, right?"

"Wow—that does sound simple," she says, barely recognizing this man she first encountered a thousand miles from here, picking fake cocaine crumbs out of his nose.

She considers the dangers of her husband's proposal, of further fusing their lives with this garbageman, who is a certifiable giant and also relapsed not too long ago, abandoning his wife and child to rekindle a love affair with alcohol and methamphetamines. A man with an actual name (Frank Spivey) who eclipsed himself with himself—and yet who, despite it all, through some spell of luck and pity, has once again come to occupy one-half of what used to be *theirs*.

"On the other hand," she says. Since his return, she hasn't observed any strangeness. No knocks on the back door followed by fifteen minutes of strained, polite conversation and unblinking eye contact. Nothing close to before, anyway. Whenever he baked the apple pie recipe she gave him, he always brought them some with vanilla ice cream and kept his visit short. Perhaps she'd over-reacted at first.

"Might've?" Vic says with a laugh.

Well, yeah, OK, even so, Heather continues. Even if there was another world in which they evicted him and his pregnant wife and their now even more enormous toddler and he found out somehow and returned from his endless bender to carry out his revenge, she was glad things had worked out the way they had: with the garbageman welcomed back by his family. Here to help Vic succor these foreclosed houses back to life on a budget.

"For the time being anyway. Not indefinitely," she says.

"Definitely not. *'Determinedly, he decided to define definitely and indefinitely the difference between the two,'* he says."

"I'm not kidding," she says.

Next night, Vic reports back on the garbageman's gratitude. "You should've seen him," he says. "At first, I thought he had spackle dust in his eye. Then a tear rolled down his face the size of a marble."

Heather closes the notebook she uses for household account-ing and removes a pair of dollar-store reading glasses and turns off the bedside lamp. "I just hope he doesn't think he's going to be here forever," she says through the dark.

"Jesus, Heather. One thing at a time—"

Now a sound radiates through the wall, and she shushes him. "You hear that?"

"Hear what?" Vic says. But the sound has already vanished, and he resumes his cryptic ritual of arranging himself for sleep, smacking and flapping the rough sheets while Heather stares at the ceiling fan, straining to listen past its chopping, blurred blades. For what she tells herself was likely a mouse nesting in the insulation in the wall. Or the crib of the garbageman's toddler's rattling under his fitful sleep. The weight of the garbageman crushing his wife's yet-again pregnant body.

You're being ridiculous, she tells herself, closing her eyes. It's like Vic said: *If he was the five-foot-tall garbageman, you wouldn't be worrying at all.*

Next morning, however, after an extra cup of coffee, Heather pulls into the colonial's driveway and comes to understand Vic's excitement with a glance. The progress since her last visit is truly staggering—what was only a disheveled colonial a couple weeks ago is not so disheveled anymore. It's quaint, really. Charming. The cracked clapboard caulked and painted. The crooked gutters cleaned and leveled out. Even the boulders that once scarred the slanting front lawn, she notices, are in the process of being repositioned into a regal rock wall.*

*Before:

After:

Heather lays on the horn, hoping to conjure her husband. To marvel at the house from the driveway with his arm wrapped around her. But after another round of honks, she only conjures the garbageman. Shirtless and grunting, he lumbers across the sun-dappled yard with another cache of stones in his bulging, tattooed arms. His long torso, straining, slick with sweat. His reddish skin slimy-looking and oddly hairless in the midmorning light. Like a skinned circus goat inked in elusive words and pictures she can't decipher:

Is that a cauldron or a bomb along his exposed abdomen?

The wing of a flapping crow or the blade of a knife up his arm?

A chest piece of a tower engulfed in flames situated before a dusky sky?

She'd met all types of freaks in her travels—homeless teens buzzing with adrenaline, who flaunted such weapons as machetes, nunchucks, ninja throwing stars. A Satanist with a tongue sliced like a serpent's. An ex-felon who, drunk on a park bench, whispered in a voice that sounded stunted from a lifetime of screaming, inviting her to look down to inspect what he'd rid himself of. And she hadn't flinched like this at the sight of any of them like she flinched now.

When the garbageman notices her, he offers her a horrible smile she can't bring herself to reciprocate. Instead she opts to remain in the safety of the car, gripping the wheel with white knuckles, waiting for him to seep back into the woods. Which he does, after depositing the stones to his pile, before dissolving back into the woods in true slasher-killer fashion—into another scene in his still unmade biopic horror feature, *The Seven-Foot-Tall Garbageman Massacre.*

She lays on the horn again, this time longer. A large crow startling from the branches of a dense pine like a shadow detaching.

She lays on the horn again. Once more. Until, finally, Vic emerges—paint-flecked and beaming—from the near-completed colonial and jogs across the yard to stick his head inside the driver side window.

"Isn't it unbelievable?" he says—just as the garbageman seeps back out of the woods, magically cleansed from the gore of the summer camp's worth of camp counselors he's just murdered with one of his large stones.

"It *is* unbelievable," she says. "That man, he's a monster!"

Vic smile widens even wider. "*Our* monster," he says.

The day he's to start the new project—the partially burnt Cape Cod—Vic stands at the sink attacking a bowl of oatmeal. Every now and then, he peers out the window, watching for the garbageman, his face glazed over with preoccupation at what he hopes to accomplish during the workday ahead, a checklist his full attention swivels inward to study. Junior, forgotten in his highchair, smearing himself with the gore of baseball-size strawberries while at the table, Heather sips her coffee, unable to reckon what has come over him.

"I'm telling you," Vic says, continuing a conversation they weren't having through a cheek taut with grains. "The man is rocket fuel for us."

But before Heather can respond, before she can ask if she might bring Junior by the Cape Cod today, the screen door of the side entrance shrieks open, and through the window, the garbageman crosses the driveway in three long strides.

Like an alarm bell, Vic's spoon rings out in his empty bowl. Suddenly, he's kissing her. He's saying goodbye, tousling Junior's hair a little too aggressively. Then he pauses at the door: "Oh, yeah, I almost forgot—don't wait up tonight. Go ahead and eat dinner without me." Owing to the longer commute, for the fore-seeable future, he'd arrive home later than usual. Around seven, maybe eight. "We need to ride this momentum until the wheels fall off."

From the window, Heather watches Vic's truck swing onto the road. A plume of dust lifting to form a haze through which she's certain she can make out the silhouette of the garbageman, sitting shotgun, his head pressed up against the ceiling of the truck's cab like a demented birthday balloon. His mouth a bear trap, opening and closing. Talking and talking. Filling her husband up with his shadow and cauldron smoke.

Then the road's empty again, and Junior falls back to his strawberries and silence. And she turns on the water and grabs a sponge to clean up what's left of Vic's oatmeal before it hardens to crust inside the bowl.

The other night, Vic told Heather how the garbageman was a talker, how he revealed his life struggles nearly every morning on their commute: "The stories are so entertaining, but so tragic!" Vic said. "*You* couldn't even dream these up. I swear to God. I told him, if this was five years ago, I'd probably have tried to write them into a screenplay," he said.

Then he told her about the garbageman's early love affair with drugs and alcohol. How his father began liquoring him up at the age of seven to make him into a fighter. How he placed bets that his son could pulverize teenagers. Adults even, once or twice. A pairing of alcohol and abuse that inevitably led him to jail, prison, and then rehab, a recurring loop that'd come to define him. Until he met his wife, started his family. Until he started working the steps in AA.

Every night, for weeks, it's another version of the same story: At dusk, Vic pulls into the driveway, where he and the garbageman proceed to stand for too long, laughing and talking as if they've forgotten their families, that they have a child apiece—the garbageman a pregnant wife. Heather watching as he towers over her husband, his shadow stabbing across the yard each time he throws his head back in laughter—a deep, guttural sound that never fails to provoke every dog within a ten-mile radius into a chorus of barks—until, finally, she has no choice and calls him inside for dinner, not wanting to be that wife, but having to be. Being forced to. Whereupon Vic proceeds to talk through hungry bites of whatever she has on rotation: chicken breast dwarfed by cucumber slices as big as CDs, onion rings you could wear like a necklace—about the day's unbelievable progress, the auspicious future of renovating foreclosed houses, one after the other into the next. Before, finally, and as always, punctuating this talk with yet another rendition of the garbageman's past, one that always leaves her second-guessing their decision to allow him to remain in their house. If the progress was worth the cost.

Otherwise, the days are quiet. Which is fine. With Junior off at kindergarten now, she works in the garden, preparing for the weekend farmer's markets. She makes phone calls regarding the latest bank short sales. She hasn't been alone like this in years, or so she thinks until the garbageman's son lets loose a howl that never fails to scare every robin from the yard, a sound that recalls to Heather her own pregnancy complications.

So, one bright morning, Heather brings the garbageman's wife a crate of fresh cauliflower. She knocks lightly at the side entrance. Then again, harder. The wind chimes tinkle overhead in the oak tree, a harmonious rubbing of notes that float into and out of each other with a unity she can't help but miss sharing with Vic.

Then a shuffling sound, a cascade of latches and locks releasing. "I'm sorry," the garbageman's wife says, rubbing her eyes. "What time is it? Was the TV too loud?"

The sunlight seems to pain her, and her baggy white T-shirt does little to diminish the enormity of the fetus swelling inside her womb. Just the glimpse dredges up the discomfort of Heather's final months carrying her normal-size son.

"I had no idea you were so far along," Heather says.

"Not really," the garbageman's wife says, and grips the door frame for balance. Already her legs have started quivering like a newborn fawn's. "Only a few months, actually."

"You're kidding."

The garbageman's wife remains silent. Maybe she hadn't heard her. When Heather asks if she's feeling all right, if she needs anything, the garbageman's wife laughs, weakly, wincing as if the uterine pressure is too much. "I'm fine," she says. Then, "No, really. Everything, I'm sure, will work out like last time." With a meek smile, she thanks Heather for the cauliflower and drifts back into the into the darkened interior of her home.

But as the days pass, Heather feels compelled to check in on her. To make a habit of pressing her ear to the bottom of a glass and listening for sounds of life, scheming up an excuse to stop by—a stray piece of mail or an old article of Junior's clothing that she already knows would never fit her toddler, another crate of vegetables from the garden. Then, upon gaining entrance and observing the ever-expanding state of her body and subsequent degradation of her home—the piled plates and overflowing hampers of clothes, the enormous toddler crashing about, knocking holes into the walls—she feels further compelled to stay and help her. To cook and clean despite the garbageman's wife's protests. To bounce that enormous child on her knee until her limbs grow weak.

"Please, you have your own life," the garbageman's wife says.

But then one afternoon, Heather's in their kitchen, washing another pile of the crusty dishes, and her worry comes to life—suddenly, the garbageman's wife cries out and Heather rushes from the sink, expecting to discover the woman split in two, her bowels strewn about the living room.

But it's only the TV. A sex scene, Heather then realizes.

Standing behind the couch, she watches two lovers twist about in the sheets. The sound of their kissing is too tender for a porno. A film noir, perhaps? No—the way the man labors over her is too familiar to lead to any sort of double-cross. A romance movie, then. But that doesn't seem right, either—as at the point of climax, the woman's as-yet-unseen face rises over the man's shoulder to reveal a Halloween mask, a grinning Jack-o-lantern with two bright-green eyes—

Then smash cut: a woman with the same eyes, only with a different man, in a different bed, TV light flickering over them. She's donned silk pajamas, but her expression's far from relaxed. Instead, she appears defeated, sunken, as a man Heather assumes to be her husband, a much more slovenly-looking man than the first, changes the channel to a horror film: a child trick-or-treating in a green witch's mask with a wart on the nose. Then the light shifts, the camera zooms, and a small smile creeps onto the green-eyed woman's face. One that disappears almost as soon as Heather notices. A romantic comedy, then, she decides.

In this way, a new routine develops—whenever Heather hears the TV, she finds herself neglecting the chores to watch movies with the garbageman's wife until Junior arrives home on the bus from kindergarten. A flow of enjoyment that waits to be disrupted by Vic's homecoming each night. At dinner, their conversation inevitably shifting toward the hardships of the garbageman's life: stories about everything from prison sentences to competitive eating contests, the unborn child he'd fathered that had killed his first wife.

However, the stories do little to humanize the man. Instead, they elevate him to a haunting in Heather's mind. One that, upon finding access to a home through a vulnerable host, threatens never to leave. It's a fear Vic confirms for her one night by suggesting they invite the garbageman and his wife over for a barbeque to show them that they aren't just tenants or employees to them, but valued friends.

"Friends?" Heather says. "I'm not sure if I'm comfortable with that—"

But she goes no further at the risk of sounding superior, and Vic says, "Well, that's unfortunate because I already asked him, Heather. I didn't think it'd be a problem, considering how much you're over there."

And so, that weekend, Heather stirs up some lemonade while Vic grills an inordinate number of hamburgers and Italian sausages that he'd bought special for the occasion. The last time he'd gone shopping, Heather couldn't tell you.

He winks at her as he sets the meat out on the patio near the garden. "I know it seems ridiculous," he says, "But you've never eaten lunch with him. You won't believe how much food he puts down."

Then, as if on cue, the side door slaps open and the garbage-man, already slick with sweat, emerges, carrying his wife's swollen body over the soft, black dirt in his tattooed arms, his boots sucking up the mud. "Every time she stands up lately, she falls over," he says, laughing. "I swear to God, you'd think *she* was the drunk."

Heather smiles. It'd be a lie to say she isn't a little curious to see how the night will progress. Both guests appear to have dressed up for this occasion. He in a paisley button-up with a few blown buttons. She in a floral-print dress, which strains to contain her enormous stomach. Heather hands each of them lemonade. They seem nervous. Jittery, even.

In a single gulp, the garbageman downs his glass and begins crunching up the ice in his teeth. She pours him another. "I just want to thank you for inviting us," he says, downing the entire glass of lemonade again.

"You're very welcome," Heather says, refilling his glass once more.

"No, I mean—" and the garbageman goes on to say that, seriously, they have no idea how grateful he is. For this second chance. For allowing him back into their home. If not for Vic and Heather, he doesn't know where his family could've gone. What he'd do. Or if he would've been able to regain control of himself at all. "We're just so lucky," he says. "So lucky. After all the misfortunes I've had. If there's ever anything I could do to pay you back."

"Nonsense," Vic says, winking again at Heather. "We're the lucky ones."

Now Heather busies herself doling out buns and salad. Waiting for the small talk to end, for the dinner conversation to begin.

To stop worrying over the entanglement of their families—and how wrong it feels, suddenly, when she considers how little Vic pays the garbageman relative to the cost of his rent.

Heather hurries to refill the garbageman's glass. Then, once more. The pitcher is almost empty now. *When will they leave?* she wonders, her gaze shifting from the garbageman to his son— who's already alarmingly taller and stronger than Junior, despite being half his age—as Junior struggles to help him turn over one of the walk's heavy flagstones in search of the salamanders nestled safe in the cool, black dirt beneath.

"No, really," the garbageman says.

Heather keeps waiting for the opportunity to ask the garbageman's wife—who'd barely touched her plate—if she feels all right, if she prefers anything else to eat. Or if she's been taking the prenatal vitamins Heather dropped off. However, between bites of a second, third, then fourth hamburger, the garbageman just keeps talking. Through hunks of meat and scraps of buns, he proceeds to issue a vivid description of the dark and proliferating energy that permeates the world. This ancient, evil smoke that drifts about, penetrating every moment. He points at an oak tree. He points at the vegetables in Heather's garden. At the darkness between the trees. With a broad, flat hand he gestures at the meadow that leads to the pond in the back. And with each motion, up from the woods, the freshly mown backyard, the black dirt in her garden, what she considered *hers*, the ancient, evil smoke seems to rise.

Nature is a natural evil, he explains. A witch's brew of mistrust that embeds itself in you. Latches on to suck at you, leaving behind only disease. Most people are miserable, a plague on this planet. The suffering of life is an incurable ailment, as far as he can see. And only a lucky few lucky souls manage to extricate themselves from the curse of living and prove exempt from such fear-based suffering.

"And you, Vic, and you, Heather," the garbageman says, his face bubbling with sweat. "You, my friends, hail from that select few." Then he rips off another half a sausage, downs his fifteenth (ish?) glass of lemonade, and says, "You're the *untouched*."

Afterward, the dishes washed and Junior put to bed, Vic and Heather sit at the kitchen table, drinking tequila on ice, the margarita mix long gone, the garbageman family still in the room with them, even if they can be heard next door, disrupting the silence with their clanging pots and pans and groaning floorboards.

"Has he been like that ever since you hired him? Is that how he usually talks to you? What did he mean when he said, 'I don't know what I would've done'?" Heather finally says.

For a while, Vic doesn't answer. Rather, he rests on the verge of speaking. At any moment she expects to hear something like: No, the garbageman usually isn't like that. Not exactly anyway. But not to worry. Like the garbageman said, he was only excited, only offering an immensity of gratitude. Instead, a scream punctures this bubble of thought.

"*Ahhhhhhhhhh!*" The sound, nowhere near as theatrical as the women in the garbageman's wife's romantic comedies, but close. There's a sudden series of knocks on the kitchen's old Dutch door that that opens onto the patio, shuddering the wood in its frame, so hard the empty glasses lining the shelves ring like a battery of off-key tuning forks. A door which, despite her pleading eyes, Vic opens, allowing the garbageman to duck inside.

"What do we owe the pleasure?" he says.

With his head pressing against the ceiling, the garbageman begins apologizing: "I'm sorry," he says. "So sorry. I don't mean to intrude." It's just that he has this idea, this idea that excites him. This new idea. Even his wife is excited about it. If they could only spare another minute of their time, he'd love to give them the rundown. Would they spare him one last indefatigable kindness?

"Let's have it," Vic says.

"A treehouse," the garbageman says through a gritted-tooth smile. "A big mother right out there in the yard." What do they think about that? For the children to grow up on. Between those two strong oak trees just outside Heather's garden. For the children, but also for them. The Greeners. To say thank you. He points out the window, frames the place where the treehouse would live with his gargantuan hands. Can't they see it already? And of course, it'd cost them nothing. He already worked everything out. A friend of his, as it turns out, had salvaged a pile of lumber that was being discarded on one of his old routes. "Pressure treated. The good stuff," he says. "The best kind."

Now Vic looks at Heather. And Heather looks back at Vic. And they look at each other. And between them looms the question of the past months while the garbageman's head, crooked and bent, continues smearing streaks of grease on the ceiling.

But Vic must've mistaken or disregarded what she's trying to convey to him with her eyes, because then he says, "Sure—why the hell not."

Next morning—Sunday—Heather stands at the kitchen window, watching the garbageman ferry lumber into the backyard. Five two-by-fours under each arm at a clip, thick stacks of plywood held overhead. More than any man should be able to carry at once. What quickly amounts to a mountainous pile of pressure-treated lumber at the foot of her garden.

At the table, Vic sips his coffee. "Well, he certainly got an early start."

Midmorning, Vic goes out to help him. Heather observes the interaction in the window: the garbageman's hands waving Vic off, and continuing to do so, dismissing him and dismissing him until Vic returns to the kitchen, laughing and arching his eyebrows.

"He's certainly persistent. He said I should spend my day off with my family. No need for me, for us, to concern ourselves."

Yet throughout the day, Heather does concern herself. Through the window, she continues to watch as the garbageman works. While Vic watches movies, a triple feature of brainless action films he'd once looked down on. Much more brainless than the garbageman's wife's taste. Through lunch, through dinner, bouncing their son on his knee, laying with him on a carpet scattered with toys as Heather listens to the garbageman's nail gun popping, his circular saw ripping through the pressure-treated boards as he begins erecting a set of steep stairs that spiral around the tree into the leafy canopy.

And sure enough, next morning, before she's even brewed the coffee, the garbageman's out there. Early. Or still. "Like he never came inside at all," she says between sips of coffee at the sink, as his nail gun continues popping. As he builds more stairs, more platforms. Erects walls. Cuts windows from which their children will supposedly wave down at them through leaves and gnarled branches before disappearing entirely into the thick billows of leaves above.

"I told you he was a hard worker," Vic says, and kisses her. It's Monday morning now. Time to leave for work. There's a foreign odor about him, of dirt and sweat, like he'd spent the night out there with the garbageman sweating, too.

At dusk, Vic's pickup pulls back in. This time, Heather observes no talking. No laughing or milling about in the drive. Instead, the garbageman beelines for the backyard and resumes working. After a fourteen-hour day, he continues, proceeding to saw and nail gun deep into the night. Building more spiral staircases, more platforms. More railings. Constructing more of his thanks via lumber, stairs, platforms, lumber, stairs, lumber, platforms—windows, plumbing, electric, dark magic, who knew what else.

Through all of this, Heather watches. Deeper into each night and into the morning. For days, she observes the treehouse taking shape between the two strong oak trees. Watches it branch and spread. Like another piece of her home that she must share. Now between a third strong oak. A fourth. Its structure growing less traditional now. Less predictable. Multilevel. Jagged, oblong. At least the parts she can see.

And each time she asks, Vic answers: "He seems fine. The kids will love it." The garbageman's wife answers more or less the same when she asks her, as well, her eyes glued to another movie, what appears to be a rom-com due to the meet-cute unfolding onscreen—a young woman in a hooptie rear-ended at a stop sign by the sports car of her future husband. Or, quite possibly, not a rom-com at all. A serial killer movie, this time, judging by the lingering vacantness in the man in the sport car's eyes.

"I don't know if I want Junior playing on that," Heather says the next morning.

"Don't worry. He really is a master carpenter," Vic says. "He's just a dedicated father who wants to build something his family can enjoy. Something in the shape of his love. To set things right. That's all. Nothing more than that. You can understand that, right?"

And it's these same sentiments each morning and every night: the family man, the dedicated father. The garbageman just trying to do what's right. On and on. And them helping him. Not to mention all their progress. Always the progress. Their golden future life.

Meanwhile, the hammering and sawing and nail gunning continues to proliferate above them. Morning, noon, and night, she hears him up there. Even when she knows the garbageman's at work with her husband, somehow, he's still there. Eclipsing what's *theirs* with his arboreal stack of small, foreclosed houses, a continuum of future and past. Sawing and nail gunning, sawing and nail gunning—until, eventually, these sounds work their way into her dreams. Into this shadowy tower of cascading pressure-treated walls that, no matter how much she might have hoped otherwise, she knew, would surely come crashing down.

At long last, quiet. That morning, the garbageman family drove off in a truck bogged down with the last of their belongings. Up until that moment they'd been fighting. Or, rather, she'd been fighting—the garbageman's wife. Screaming her blame at him like the monster they always assumed *he* was. If he'd been five inches shorter, or if she'd been five inches taller, Heather would've called the police countless times already. Instead, she purchased a white-noise machine, so Junior wouldn't hear the curses hurled against their walls, and hunkered down for a few weeks until their year-long lease ran out.

But, now, yes: quiet—a quiet so anticipated Heather can barely focus on the book she's reading—a quiet that makes every sound louder: the hush of Junior sleeping on the monitor, the jingle of ice each time Vic tips back his drink, the summer breeze that presses on the ancient glass of the bedroom's double-hung windows. It doesn't matter. Her distraction is her own, not *theirs* now.

"Mind if I watch TV?" says Vic.

"Knock yourself out, doc." It'd been a while, and Heather had worn the green silk nightie figuring tonight would be the night they consummated their newfound privacy. But if Vic wanted to watch TV, if that's how he intended to enjoy the house's quiet, she didn't mind.

He settles on a horror film—some sequel of a sequel of a summer camp slasher from the eighties. Which surprises her. As a rule, Vic turns his nose up at genre. He thinks the real world is strange enough. *Maybe he recognizes the actress on screen?* That hot little number. Whose pale breasts now bounce about in a low-cut silver party dress as she runs, moonlit, screaming along a dark tunnel of trees. Maybe she'd been in his acting class? Maybe he'd fucked her. Had he fucked her? For a laugh—or perhaps in hopes of jumpstarting some passion—she turns to ask him then reconsiders, owing to the seriousness dragging at his face. A look he's worn ever since the cracks in the garbageman's life grew too obvious to ignore, the treehouse too large, a literal shantytown overhead growing to resemble the madness contained within his mind.

Vic tilts back the rest of a drink, the ice knocking against his teeth. Blue TV light playing in the hollows of his eyes.

Heather lifts the book, resumes reading. Or tries to. Her eyes moving across the words without really digesting them. Reading, then rereading—because, my God, what a set of pipes that actress has! Followed by the *shing* of a long knife. The killer must've caught her. Her disembowelment must've begun.

Heather lowers her book, expecting to see the actress reduced to a bloody heap of bleached-blonde hair and tanned flesh, and is surprised that she hasn't been. That on screen, the actress appears unbloodied and perfectly alive. Still in that party dress—in a cabin with her drunk friends and letterman boyfriend. The windows appear reinforced with sheets of plywood and random boards. Only there's a problem: While she sits on the couch in a state of shock—a flannel blanket slung over her—her mouth isn't screaming. Even as Vic lifts the remote and turns down the volume—her scream continues: barking and soaring about the bedroom, like no scream Heather's heard before. But if not the TV or the garbageman's wife, then who's screaming it?

A half hour later, a squad car pulls up. Heather and Vic unlock the front door and hurry outside to meet the officer, leaving Junior sleeping in his bedroom. A shadow emerges, which clarifies into a young man almost as short as the garbageman's wife.

He clicks on a flashlight, begins casting the beam about the trees like he might discover the source of the scream there. "Have you heard anything else since you called?" he says.

"Still just the one long scream," Heather says, trying to keep herself covered with the bathrobe she'd hastily thrown over herself. "The entrance to the apartment's over here. Just around this side."

As he follows them around the house, Vic remains silent, the ice jingling in his glass—down the path of flagstones the garbageman had laid for them to the side entrance, a door the garbageman had painted a tasteful, glossy barn red.

"And you heard nothing else?" the officer says in a voice shaky with excitement. "A truck pull up? The screen door smacking open and shut? Did you hear him walking around the house at all? A guy that size in a house as old as this—you would've heard him, right?"

Heather answers no, no, no, and yes: they would've heard him, without a doubt, the house had been so quiet all night. The hardwood floors are so thin, she says. At night, the house creaked with the rhythm of his breathing.

At this, the officer's face drops, his shoulders slouch. Probably, he hadn't gone on many calls, hadn't experienced the action he'd sought upon joining the small-town police force. "I'd guess it was an animal, then," he says, his scuzzy mustache barely registering in the moonlight.

"I'm not sure. We've been here for almost five years and I've never heard anything like that," Heather says.

"Sometimes an animal takes that long to come around." But even so, the officer says, he doesn't want them to think he'll take their safety for granted. That's his sole concern, what he's pledged to protect with his life. Yes, tonight, he's hunting big game, and he promises to hunt until the threat of the big game is neutralized. He'll wait out in the squad car all night, if he has to. He'll sit in a chair outside their bedroom while they sleep. He directs this last part at Vic, who passes the question to Heather with a shrug.

"Let's just start with the house, then," she says. And the officer throws open the screen door of the side entrance with so much force it slaps against the house. So hard the ice in Vic's glass jumps. But there's no time to check on him—the officer hurls himself into the dark of the garbageman's side of the house, the beam of his flashlight scrubbing the room in a frenzy.

When Heather flips on the lights, the officer sighs at the absence of blood in the hallway. There's none in the living room, either. From room to room, they move, flipping on the lights. But there isn't a sign of struggle anywhere. No garbageman or his wife or gigantic toddler—unless you know what to look for:

The greasy marks left by his hair whenever he ducked through a doorway, for example. Or the dents in the floor from the feet of the armchair he sat in. The adult-size bite marks left by his giant toddler. Not to mention, whatever jagged shiv the whole garbageman saga had broken off in her husband—who still stands near the door, nursing his drink, and ghost white.

"Okay—so that's all?" says Heather.

"I guess so," says the officer.

"An animal, then."

"That's what I'd put my money on."

"An animal, then," she repeats—because the officer seems reticent to go. Maybe, somehow, in his mind, the seven-foot-tall garbageman would spring out from around the corner to settle his score and he'd dispense of the garbageman with his service revolver.

"Okay—I can live with that," she continues, and still the officer doesn't budge. She flips off the lights, hoping he'll get the message. Eager as she is to return to the new privacy of her house. That lush quiet. To allow the whole garbageman nightmare to sink into the past. She opens the door and pushes Vic outside with the palm of her hand.

"Hang on a minute," the officer says. "What's this?"

"What's what?" Heather says, turning back.

Aiming his flashlight, the officer identifies his concern: what appears to be nothing but the antique wallpaper that covers much of the house—until he switches his flashlight back off. And there on the hallway wallpaper hover two points of light, about five feet up. He flips his flashlight on and jiggles the beam over them, making the points of light disappear and reappear. Then he clomps over to the wall opposite the points of light and crouches.

"Is that your downstairs bathroom?" he says, pressing his eye against the wall.

"My what?"

"Come here," he says.

Heather does, placing her eye where the officer had placed his. The darkness snapping away into a light that initially blinds her. One that soon clarifies into her bathroom, her toilet, the claw-footed bathtub where she bathes herself and her five-year-old son.

"I don't understand," she says. But of course she does—or, rather, understands what the officer's suggesting. That he'd been watching her. Or, judging by the height of the peepholes, she had been. Watching them. But that can't be right, either. That'd be absurd.

She looks at Vic, and he looks back at her, the question of the moment hanging between them like swamp gas until, from a little further down the hallway, the officer calls out to them in a voice quivering with glee, "Is that your son sleeping in there?"

A few days later, they hear the long scream again, coming from the mossy clearing in the trees behind the house. Like the garbageman's wife being murdered, over and over again. Except that's impossible now.

If not that, what then? A coyote? A lost fawn? The squall of a horny house cat? In bed Heather connects to the dial-up and clicks through a catalog of online animals, trying to match her memory of the sound with that made by her laptop's tinny speaker.

"Not that. Not that, either," she says. A fisher cat shrieks from her lap. Repeatedly. But, while not unlike the garbageman's wife being murdered, the shriek isn't quite human, either. Not exactly. "But who knows what sounds an animal might make in the throes of passion?"

"I wouldn't worry," Vic says.

Heather runs a hand beneath the sheets, grating her nails across Vic's wiry down of chest hair. "I wasn't serious," she says. Just the opposite, in fact. The house is *theirs* again, and returning to the other half of their home feels like going somewhere, a vacation destination inside their very own house.

Now Vic excuses himself to shuffle off down the hallway again. His footsteps stopping briefly where Heather hung the sofa art that morning—a snow-draped barn—to cover one of the many peepholes the officer so joyously pointed out. Before continuing to the kitchen again, the liquor cabinet he stripped that summer with the tick infestation. The summer they created the chicken salad game.

Remember the chicken salad game? Heather thinks.

With a jingle of ice Vic returns to lie atop the comforter. Silent and sweating. Tequila-breathed as usual these days, his odorous mouth partially pried and poised for what she worries will become talk of his failure to protect them again. His abdication of duty. A series of excuses that'd begin like, "There's no way she could've done all that, Heather. We would've heard her drill. Even over the usual racket. The peepholes must've been hidden there all along."

A relentless hedging that'd eventually give way to apologies and self-pity: "I'm sorry," he'd say. "I lost track of things. I had nothing but money signs for eyes."

But tonight, thankfully, no—Vic flips the TV off and proceeds, yet again, to knock the ice in his drink against his teeth at short intervals. As outside, the silence waits for another shriek to split it, and Junior whimpers on the monitor in the throes of a dream. And sleep finds them, without them having sex again—another night to add to their months-long dry patch, when they'd never gone more than three days, historically, before the garbageman moved in.

Next morning, Heather's back over in the empty half of their home. Where the garbageman or the garbageman's wife—apparently—drilled these peepholes in the antique wallpaper. Leveled their hidden gaze at them through the beautiful, frenzied blossoms that graced the wall dividing the house. A series of eyes that they utilized to watch them eat, shit, and not fuck. Kiss their son goodnight. And who knew what else?

Despite the peepholes' near invisibility, Vic wants to patch everything. Even with the garbageman family gone, she had to fight Vic these last couple days into not peeling off the elegant wallpaper, not ruining it by spackling over the holes. "I insist," she said. "If you think I'll end up watching you, we'll just hang artwork. We'll hang photographs everywhere."

Now Heather picks up another art piece, looks at it. This framed daguerreotype of a dour-faced wedding. See that other hole over there? She taps a hanger in and hangs it: The strangers stare back at her with silver eyes, already sullen in their marriage.

Then, here they are again—in bed and not touching. Vic's expression not too far off from that silver groom. They listen to the bullfrogs and peepers in the swamp, who still sound so much louder. A summer wind on the windows. Junior's gentle murmurs, dreaming restlessly on the monitor. The ice knocking against Vic's teeth, his tequila mouth poising and unpoising to talk—

Only this time he does: "We would've sensed her, Heather. I'm sure of it. You saw how eager that cop was, he was horny to find some crime. So horny he'd invent it. 'Hunting the big game.' Who talks like that? I'm telling you: We would've felt her eyes on us. The previous owner bore those holes. Or if not him, someone else. An electrician, perhaps—after a mouse chewed into and shorted a wire."

Meanwhile, Heather mouths right along with him in the dark.

A package arrives the next morning. As Vic stabs at his oatmeal and Junior sits quietly at the table, eating strawberries, Heather rips open the cardboard box. A motion-sensor camera she mail-ordered out of a B&H catalog. With night vision and extended battery life, a small screen for instant playback. She holds it up for her son, waiting in vain for him to react.

"See what mommy bought!?" she says.

"He sees," Vic says. Then, "You sure we can afford that?"

"After the year we had?" Heather says with a laugh.

Vic shakes his head, doesn't offer her a kiss before he drives off with Junior for drop off. Leaving her to carry her new camera into the woods, to a clearing bearded with comfortable moss. Where she straps the camera to a diseased oak riddled with lumps and carefully adjusts the shot.

Back at the house she spends the rest of the day hanging more sofa art: a thickly painted hunting lodge, an orchard strung with pink blobs, a flock of sailboats bending over on a windy lake. Stuff she'd bought at an estate sale. Until dinner.

"Remember the chicken salad game we used to play?" she says, standing at the counter, struggling to slice an heirloom tomato the size of a cannonball with a kitchen knife.

Vic sits at the table, still in his painter whites—flecked with the off-white of the disheveled colonial he'd yet to finish since the garbageman left. He scoops a whole grain cracker through the deep bowl she'd made in hopes of jogging his memory. "What game, again?" he says. "When you made up those backstories for me?"

Frowning, Heather watches him chew.

He chews just like the deer she watches on the camera's playback the next morning. Skittish, like a predator might be lurking just out of view. Even though he knows the threat is gone. *Neutralized.* My poor husband, she thinks.

Now, as she crouches there in the clearing, the herd parades across the frame at 10x speed in grainy green with undeserved majesty. Her muck boots sinking ever-so-slowly into the moss. "Mange with legs," she hears her stepfather say, what he used to call them. "Mutant dogs."

She deletes the deer, repositions the camera. Curses under her breath the entire walk back to the house.

Every morning that week, it's the same story—out the back door, through the silvery grass and stinking dead leaves into the shadowy trees, where the camera sits waiting. She tries everything: heaps of vegetables, birdseed. Lunch meat. The dry oatmeal she buys for Vic's health. But only deer come to this party, these eighty-pound ticks with green-glow eyes—her stepfather's tormentors now her own.

A part of her wishes she hadn't sold his stockpile of guns. A part of her wishes she had a stick of dynamite. A part of her wishes that her stepfather might be momentarily risen back to life to answer one question: *Old and ugly man, how can I draw this mysterious animal back to me out of the night?* before being shot dead again.

She's just left the hardware store one day when she gets the idea—as if he'd whispered the answer to her question, hot and soft in her ear. She pulls up to a blood-matted raccoon carcass on the shoulder of the road, its yawning mouth dried up stiff with her stepfather's words: "Take me with you!"

So, of course she does. Carefully, she shovels its body into the bed of the truck. Drives home with the sick-sweet taste of the animal hovering in the cab and lays the carcass in the clearing upon the moss, laughing to herself. As per the instructions. Thinking, *no, Vic, my fragile little flower, everything is going absolutely all right.* "Just peachy," she says to herself.

But in the days to follow, the reeking raccoon only sinks deeper into itself, grows laden with flies. Meanwhile, it's the same deer, the same incremental work of reinhabiting the side of the house, the same nightly ritual of her brooding, possibly alcoholic husband, followed by the same silence—and no sex.

"How long are you going to mope around like this?" she says amid another touchless night. "For Christ's sake, forgive yourself—what sane person would've anticipated any of this? Who could've pegged those two as crazed voyeurs willing to drill peepholes into walls? Even with all their red flags? No one, doc. If there's a lesson to be learned here, I, for one, don't care to learn it. And you shouldn't, either." Can't they just move on? The heavier furniture needs to come up from the basement—the oak desk, the swivel chair. She needs, *they* need an office to work. For their businesses. How are they ever going to finish the Colonial and discover their next flip house? How will she sell her vegetables at more farmer's market? Or does he want to go back to simply painting houses? Pilot season is approaching, and maybe he's thinking he'll fly back West?

"Dear God, no," Vic says. "Please stop." He stares into the ceiling fan and sips at another sweating drink. "Okay, okay— tomorrow, I promise. I'll come home during lunch."

"Good," Heather says. "We can make chicken salad and play our game."

"What game?" he says.

"You'll have to find out."

Heather rises early the next morning to watch the playback—the same collapsed raccoon, the deer parade. *Blah blah blah*—until, there, another raccoon lumbers across the ghastly infra-green frame. And boy it's big. It orbits the dead one, then leans in and hugs it, seeming to whisper sweet raccoon nothings into its ear.

The sight causes Heather's own ears to tickle. Goose-bumps to ripple along her bare arms. The camera's playback is soundless. But before dismounting, you can see the mouth of the live raccoon form an upturned flute on the little screen, no doubt, issuing an operatic sound, a declaration of its passion and love.

Back at the house, Heather connects to the internet to search *Raccoon Necrophilia Sound*. She comes up empty. However, there happen to be a few articles about the phenomenon. One by one, she clicks them open, impatiently waiting for the websites to load.

Apparently, she comes to learn, it isn't unusual among the species. Not at all. She isn't surprised. Come to think of it, Heather's never been surprised once in her life. Not even when she discovered the peepholes. Not when she told Vic she was pregnant just a few months after reappearing in his life. Or when he dropped to his knee to beg her to marry him. Not when a vein exploded in her stepfather's stomach and blood shot across the room from his large mouth. Or even when her mother died slowly, not two years after Junior's birth, with none of the tough grit she exhibited throughout her life. Concerned? Maybe. But surprised? Heather? Never once.

She plugs the laptop into the printer, clicks *PRINT*. And soon, a page of thick, sheeny photography paper rolls out like a slow tongue. She holds it up in the morning sunlight.

Like a Harlequin novel, she thinks. Like a scene straight out of *Days of our Lives*.

Chicken salad for lunch again. Heather holds out the photograph. "Check this out," she says.

Vic stares at the raccoons for a long time with this nonexpression that tells her he doesn't grasp the vacant gaze of the dead raccoon beneath. A plaque of crackers and chicken salad coats his sudden smile.

"I love it," he says, before Heather can explain anything. Before she can express the ways in which natural instincts—such as earning money—can sometimes lead to maladaptive behavior in the artificial world we live in. But Vic's smitten. He loves the photograph so much he wants to hang it on the wall of their new office. "Right now," he tells her.

"I'll slip it into a frame, then." Heather wraps the chicken salad up and puts it in the refrigerator, then follows him upstairs. Leaning the newly framed photograph against the wall, she tells him to take off his clothes and lie down naked on the floor. He obliges. She strips down as well and mounts him, her body warped and ghostlike in the reflection of the glass that encloses the photograph of the raccoons. He reaches up for her, the floor creaking steadily beneath her knees. Then creaking faster. Until

her husband starts grunting away, like a drowning victim sputtering back to life. And only then, in this sudden spasm, does Vic
seem to remember: the chicken salad game they used to play.
How they agreed the flavor of the lunch was so improved by the
appetite they'd worked up in the bedroom. In his wide, orgas-
ming eyes, she sees all this very clearly. And both of them come
very much alive.

Afterward, Vic helps her carry up the oak desk and swivel
chair from the basement. He hangs the photograph on the wall
where they can always see it.

He starts spending his nights in there, thinking about their
house and how to further improve it—maybe a small farm for
them in the backyard, he calls her in to suggest one night. To
compliment her garden. Suddenly, he doesn't think chickens and
goats are such a bad idea. He wants to purchase a purebred grey-
hound pup from a neighbor. He wants to buy an apartment
building. Wants to travel the world—to go anywhere, everywhere. He wants to have another child. No, two more children.
Three.

"Are you serious?" Heather says.

"I've never been more serious in my entire life."

Heather laughs—because she told him at the jump. From the
moment they decided to go ahead with the pregnancy. Lying atop
the twin size back at the Oakwood, she said: If she had this child,
it would be their only focus. Just it. Her heart, she knew, was too
intense and loyal for another, that at that volume, her love
couldn't be distributed evenly. If her heart grew too bloated, she'd
end up having to choose between the children. A fact perhaps
more gruesome than what lonely raccoons do to dead ones in the
night. But no less true. No less gruesome. "Do you remember me
saying any of this?" she asks him.

"Not at all," he says, laughing as they lie there, enjoying the breeze from the ceiling fan. Enjoying a quiet that makes her want to jump him again. And maybe again the next morning. And again after that.

In this fashion, life resumes. Soon, it's like the garbageman never existed, never happened at all—Vic coming when she calls from wherever he is inside the house, looking at her without looking past her now. He forgives himself. Before bed, he runs his fingers through her hair like he used to. Whispers dirty things to her like she likes. He stops drinking so much. Marches around the yard with Junior, turning over rocks in search of worms and bugs.

When she can't sleep, sometimes, she comes in here: the office, a glass of tequila in her hand. To sit in the chair and contemplate that moment when she saw what it was. Over and over. That realization. The moonlight over that mossy clearing, now blazing so perfectly upon the photograph's surprise. What's so easy to forget. To not celebrate. The mystery of the natural world. The way people are. Across her brain, she does this, again and again. Like a savory flavor on her tongue. A truth she always seems able to recall the moment she stares into this other creature's eyes.

HOUSE OF THE VULTURE

Now Junior works with his father—instead of playing modified football or baseball after school, skateboarding on the curb behind the Quick Stop with his friends—every weekday (and some weekends) until the sun dips beyond the onion fields and the migrant shanties illuminate the black dirt's rim on his parents' latest renovation: this secluded farmhouse with only one neighbor and syringes and beer cans ground way down in the dirt of the overgrown yard.

For his first job, Junior must rake this yard clean, so as not to ruin the mower's blade, his father explains, while he attempts to tame the unruly grass.

Without a break, Junior rakes for hours. The way the tines of the rake snag on the knotted grass and detritus the previous owners left behind proves exhausting. When the elderly neighbor drives by in his rusty pickup and waves, Junior can't even lift his arms.

A week passes until, finally, his father deems the yard clean enough to set him loose with the push mower. But no more than five minutes after his father pulls the pull start, the mower jumps from Junior's grip as if ripped away from him by the hand of a demon. Then, blue smoke and a smoldering smell. The mower on its back. Its blade a bent propeller slowing to a stop.

"Looks like you caught a stray shotgun shell," his father says, stooping to admire the small crater in the grass. He picks up the twisted casing and pockets it. Then he stands up and tousles Junior's hair, smiling a real face-buster of a smile—like Junior's just been baptized into something distinctly *Greener.* "Do me a favor, will ya? Don't mention this to your mother if she stops by."

In the meantime, Junior's handed a scythe from out of one of the rotten barns. "Like this." His father demonstrates for him, swinging the blade a few times through the grass before disappearing back into the farmhouse.

Alone now, Junior swings the scythe, lopping off swaths of grass. As the curved and rusted blade sings through the air, a large vulture appears, pinwheeling overhead. Junior stops to watch it—a small speck that causes his neck hairs to rise in a chorus to hit a chilling note.

Not that Junior believes in omens or ghosts. But there's something about the inside of the farmhouse he doesn't like: the way the previous owner's keys still hang from the rack, their dirty clothes still mashed in the hampers. The shattered microwave contains the dried-out husks of four gas station burritos, and stagnant water fills the sink. "Don't mention this to your mother, son," his father said.

No matter how Junior figures—there's only one place the family could've gone without their belongings like that. And then, another worry: If they hadn't all perished, what would happen if the surviving family members came back to reclaim what they'd lost?

"You really don't know what happened to them?" he asks his father one day out on the still-unruly lawn. But before he can answer, his mother's tires crunch on the gravel drive and his father disappears back into the farmhouse with his flashlight. Too eager to wait to greet her, the same way he's too eager to wait for O & R to flip the electric on so he can fully see what he's getting done. The past few days, he's been working in the dark.

A door slams and his mother emerges from the side of one of the dilapidated barns. Arms straining with swollen bags from

Lowe's, she duckwalks toward him. Or, at least, in his direction—because she only offers him a smile before plunging into the farmhouse after his father.

Junior stands in the choppy lawn, watching after them. Nose itching with the breeze, fear sinking in his chest like a stone settling into the murk of a pond. Every now and then, he catches his father's flashlight's beam dusting at another dark window and feels better at the sign of life. Other times he hears his mother's laughter. Usually such a light-hearted sound. Then she emerges from the farmhouse, toting something, his father right behind her, toting something too. A process they repeat, laying the items in the yard:

A sun-bleached suitcase.

An armful of embossed pint glasses.

Clothes Swiss-cheesed by moths.

A swivel chair speckled with white mold.

A plastic bin stuffed with electric and tax bills.

A cardboard box full of personal belongings—

An accumulation that his mother soon leaves the rotation to poke through in the small section of lawn Junior had managed to mow before the mower blew up. As the vultures spiral overhead like a horde of hungry spirits, homing in to peck at these scraps and decide what's truly garbage and what might be worthy of ingesting. Again and again, his father emerges to spill more scraps for her. Like offerings. Fragments of the previous owner's lives that Junior cannot seem to stitch together into a reason for leaving them behind.

"What happened here?" his mother says, reading his mind. Or more precisely, reading the words in his mind—because she's not inquiring about the previous owners, but the bowl of dirt the shotgun shell's explosion had made. Junior shrugs, giving away nothing, as per his father's request.

He now appears, carrying a cardboard box labeled *Hallow-een Decorations*. "Find any treasure out here?" he says.

"Not as far as you're concerned," Junior's mother says.

"To the dump then?"

"To the dump!" she says as Junior continues to observe the vultures churn in the sky above them, blanketing them with stale air and bad tidings. His parents' excitement: just another item on the list of things he can't seem to comprehend.

With the remains deemed worthless, Junior helps his father dump them without ceremony into the sagging trailer hitched to the rear of his truck. The well-worn clothes and moldy chairs some-one once sat in, watching bad TV. The notebooks penned in a desperate scrawl. Memories that'd never be read again. Now only so much garbage. "You sure we shouldn't save any of this?" Junior says.

His father shrugs, disappears into the farmhouse again as his mother, reading the disappointment on his face, stops picking through the scraps long enough to offer a small condolence. "Don't worry," she says. "These people aren't coming back."

"Why not?" he almost says—too afraid of the length and detail with which his mother might answer. In silence, he resumes swinging his scythe, his attention oscillating between his father's/mother's rhythms and the vultures accumulating in the sky. He tries counting them:

Twenty-five . . .

Twenty-six . . .

Twenty-seven—

But he keeps losing count and starting back up again, unable to add it all up. Instead, he tries to focus on the whistle the sharpened blade makes. On the satisfaction of stepping into another clear swatch, slicing more yellowing grass away. On his family's slow and steady colonizing of this broken place. But after a while, his curiosity proves too much, and he gestures to his father, who's struggling a torn ottoman from the trash heap toward the trailer:

"Were those here when we arrived?" he says.

"Were what here?" his father says. He laughs. "I think you've been watching too many horror films, son." And his mother, still there picking through the few remaining items, laughs, too, joining her musical eeriness with his father's gruff chugging, sending it upward into the ever-growing horn of vultures. An instrument that seems to amplify their laughter, striking a key that doesn't bode well. Especially from his mother.

"Junior, come quick!" his mother says from inside one of the barns, and he drops his scythe and runs to save her. Understanding that the bad omen of this place has now been realized. That the ground has given and she now lies broken at the bottom of a forgotten well. Or a beam has fallen. A rattlesnake slithered out from the darkness and struck her.

Turns out, his mother had only found evidence that a person had made a home out of the barn. Inside, her flashlight beam crawls over an old box-spring mattress, a refrigerator full of skunked beer, a crumpled pair of diabetic socks. She laughs. "Looks like the wife must've kicked her husband out!"

Junior musters a laugh. Though he's unable to see what's so enjoyable about the way previous tenants lived their lives. Same with the picture his mother then proceeds to paint for him: the thirty-beer a day habit. His conservative news-watching on the small rabbit-ear in the corner, the electric heater the cast-out spouse used to warm his toes. The way his wife took up with another man inside, leaving the windows open so he could hear them at night. On and on.

"You can almost still feel him in here, muttering under his breath," she says.

"Okay—no more ghost stories!" says his father, who'd apparently been standing in the doorway, observing them: "*Hep-hep-hep*—there's no money in standing around!" He claps at them until they start moving out the door.

Junior spends the rest of the afternoon stuffing the room's contents into garbage bags and loading them into the trailer until its tires need a refill of air before the drive to the dump. On the way, he tries to rearticulate his concern to his father. How did his mother know these things about the man who lived in the barn? And what about the vultures?

But his father's never had any patience for Junior's *fictions,* as he often called them. His mother's yarns. To pacify Junior, his father tells him not to worry, continually rerouting the subject back to the renovation of the farmhouse—their plans to sister in a beam before knocking out a loadbearing wall, to jackhammer a window into the stone foundation because the kitchen doesn't get enough sun. To fix the mower to better tame the lawn.

"Listen here," he says. "I'm trying to teach you how to do something. Something applicable in terms of living a comfortable life. Something that took me too long to realize." He chucks a thumb over his shoulder, gesturing back toward the loaded trailer they towed. "Do you want to end up like these people, son?"

He talks like this until they pull into the dump. Where, giddy now, he jumps from the truck to unload the trailer: a medley of musty mattress, messes of clothes, and pregnant garbage bags. A dented projector television. Stacks of photo albums, journals in milk crates.

"Hey, maybe let's hang on to that," Junior says.

"Hang on to what?" his father says, obviously having heard him, but hurling the milk crate of journals into the mountain of trash anyway.

He laughs and laughs, his father. Garbage juice leaks down Junior's arm while he hops away to joke with the dump attendant— an older man with a constant wet cough, a perpetual cigarette cupped in one hand. His father knows him from years of the same exchanges. "Rico, baby. How's la familia?" he says.

"Still waiting on your autograph," Rico says. "My girlfriend and I saw you on TV the other day. On this late-night horror movie." He snaps his fingers, thinking: "*The Runestone*, it was called. You got speared by a monster with a rusted spike, man!"

"Must've been someone else," his father says with a wink. "I always thought horror was beneath me." Then they drive back to the farmhouse, Junior thinking about all the things they never talk about, and the cycle begins again.

In coming days, Junior throws away the burrito husks, the shattered microwave itself. He throws away dog-eared books with notes scrawled in the margins. More dirty clothes mashed in the hampers. More blankets, pillows. Crucifixes. Sheets stained with what might be blood. "Tomato sauce," his father corrects.

Junior wishes his mother would stop by more often. But she appears sporadically, and at random, with dirt from her garden caked on the knees of her jeans. For a while there, she makes a project of scrubbing the granite countertops in the kitchen, trying to salvage them with bleach, her hands reddened and chapping, before disappearing again.

One day, she takes a dump trip with them.

In the yard before leaving, she smiles at Junior standing by the piled trailer with the scythe. "My little grim reaper," she says. They drive to the dump, three across, with Junior in the middle, listening to their chatter: his father talking about what's still to be done to the house, and his mother, ignoring this, responding with whatever grabbed her:

The reason the house held so many crucifixes. (A Catholic mother.)

The stains on the counter. (They cooked spaghetti with marinara to stay on a budget.)

How they ended up in the farmhouse in the first place. (A family inheritance from the Catholic mother.)

It's a series of his mother's "yarns" that his father now seems to tolerate. Because the dump meant happy times. The dump meant joy and sunny skies, and a pair of spotted fawns plucking and chewing up daisies. The dump meant progress and curiosity, a fusion of his parents, who reach across him to touch one another, smiling soft smiles.

After pulling through the weigh station, his father throws the truck into reverse, and Rico guides them to a spot in the large hanger.

"Heather, my love!" And his mother embraces Rico like an old friend as his father begins unloading the trailer, dashing the last of the previous owners across the hanger's filthy concrete floor. An expanse that gives way to cliffs of endless garbage as Junior stands there, watching the bulldozer in the distance crush a pile of couches toward a large container, trying to see what his parents see.

"You gonna help us with this or what?"

His mother slips a gloved hand over his shoulder. "We lose you again, son?" And his father slips a gloved hand around her waist. They stand there like that for a moment, a family, admiring the hydraulic scoop of the bulldozers as they rip into the wood and foam and spring of one of their discarded couches.

"Okay—this trailer isn't gonna finish unloading itself," his father finally says.

He's afraid to salvage anything in secret. In case his father decides to check his pockets and accuse him of going against the philosophy of "throw anything of zero value away." Anything wooden, he's been instructed to smash into a twisted mound with a large sledgehammer his father removes from his truck to be burned later in a bonfire, he explains—which will save them a pretty penny in dump fees.

With each swing, the crooked furniture and dressers splinter apart like an explosion of wings as the pile grows around him. Late afternoon, when the elderly neighbor drives by, waving again, Junior finds himself stronger now. This time his arms aren't too tired to wave back.

In a dark corner of the furnace room, he discovers an electric organ that his father helps him load into the truck. At the dump, Rico plugs the instrument into a socket, discovers its pipes are still working. The few test notes he plays echo masterfully over the garbage while the bulldozers chew and plow. "I used to play at Sunday service," Rico says.

It gets so Rico plays what Junior recognizes as a funeral dirge whenever they pull up. An ominous blend of the same three notes. Not exactly a catchy tune. But after so many trips, it lodges itself in Junior's head until he'd give anything for the triad to relent. His mother must've caught the bug on one of her visits too, because she starts humming the song one day while working to revive the kitchen. "Where'd you hear that?" Junior says.

"Beats me," she says.

Now Junior's clearing the last of the bedrooms, trying not to hum this melody while he works and failing. The girl's room confuses him—a bizzarro version of his own, complete with the same band posters, the same corkboard tacked with scribbled notes from friends. Skateboarding stickers: *Thrasher, Vans, Tilt-Mode, Volcom.* The same strings of Christmas lights hung arbitrarily around the room, as if she, too, were afraid of the dark. The only difference: the spray-painted marijuana leaves, the penises, the swastika markered in the closet. At which even his mother shakes her head, unwilling to throw her imagination into this past.

Had this girl gone to his middle school?

Had she passed him in the halls?

Junior can't remember any candlelight vigils or car wrecks. Can't remember any reports of disappearances in the news, any pictures on milk cartons. *Or have I only forgotten?* he thinks, loading the last of these contents into the trailer.

His father drives them all on a final trip to the dump. Where Rico plays his usual accompaniment—the same three notes— while the last of the farmhouse's contents are plowed, crushed, lost in the mountainous structure of trash. After unloading, his mother kisses Rico a wet goodbye, one on each cheek, and his father pumps Rico's hand. Before Rico, instead of the dirge, plays them out with a hymnal, a soulful, joyous sound as his parents wave goodbye.

"Stop for hamburgers?" his father says on the way back to the farmhouse.

"Turkey burgers," his mother says, and taps her heart.

Next day, back in the yard, Junior swings his scythe. It's breezy today, the still-accumulating vultures higher up. Across the road, an army of migrants bend, harvesting onions. While his father's tools rip and bang inside the farmhouse, the air causes hot tears to drip and roll down his cheeks like embers.

A horn blares from the road, startling him. There a truck idles, inside of which the elderly neighbor sits, an alligator-skin cowboy hat on his head, an oxygen mask strapped over his face. Slowly, he cranks the window down and slides the mask to one side and begins speaking through a gray, puckered mouth, inaudible at this distance. He holds something out—a slice of lemon, Junior realizes after walking up to the truck.

"It'll help with the tearing," the old man says, and introduces himself: "George. I've been mowing this unruly place for decades." He points across the road.

Junior thanks him, puts the slice inside his mouth. He takes the slice back out.

"You gotta leave it in your mouth, son," George says.

"I'm just curious about something," Junior says. "About what happened here? In this house?" he says.

"Happened?"

"To the previous owners. Did they die?"

"Die? Hell no," George says, a wheeze in his laugh. "They moved into those new apartments downtown. What the hell made you think something like that?" He shakes his head at the thought. Then George slides his oxygen mask back over his face and drives off, without waiting for him to answer.

It gets so Junior starts seeing things. At work or back home in the garden with his mother, picking the vegetables for the Sunday farmer's market. At dinner when his father complains about the diet she's now imposed on him. Out of the corner of his eye he catches these dead-alive folks everywhere—specters on the cusp of approaching him to make him answer for what he's done.

Superstitions develop quickly. Throughout each day, Junior tries and fails not to hum the funeral dirge around his father. It's a constant effort. Between the vultures and the previous owners and this melody, it all adds up to approaching horrors.

In time, the farmhouse is cleaned out and emptied. The renovations are underway now. The yard clean, the house nearly painted. The toilet capable of flushing without backing up. His mother not coming by as much anymore, if at all.

In the freshly scythed yard, his father hands him a can of gasoline, some matches. "Remember that twisted mound of furniture that you sledgehammered apart?" (He says this as if the next task promises to be just as fun.) And for the rest of the day, Junior tends the bonfire he makes, biting a lemon and poking at these last smoldering remnants with his scythe, the wood charring and spitting sap until, finally, giving into the fire and ash.

He glances up past the farmhouse, at the black tornado of birds that still churns above. Their numbers are fewer today, or so it seems. To double-check, he begins counting: nine, ten, eleven, twelve, thirteen . . .

A breeze kicks up, shuffles across the mown grass to pluck a single ember up from the blaze. Junior watches the ember—this very last piece of the previous family's lives, the air seeming to flux around it, huffing like a lung before releasing the ember atop the cedar shake roof of one of the barns. Where it disappears completely. Then reappears, smoking. At first it's only as big as the tip of a lit cigarette. Then larger.

The smile vanishes from Junior's face. "Dad, Dad, Dad, Dad, Dad, Dad!" he calls, and keeps calling. Until his father emerges from the farmhouse, shaking his head with annoyance.

"Now what—" But then he notices—the swirling black smoke, and snaps into action: running off to return with a twenty-eight-foot ladder hoisted above his head, then extending the rungs and angling a path for himself up into the flames.

With deft speed, he runs off again to turn on the spigot and unspool a length of hose. He begins climbing—faster than Junior has seen him move before. Water splashing down in arrhythmic spurts from above. His father's boots on the second-to-top rung. His head out of sight over the apex of the roof as he shouts: "Brace the ladder, son!"

For minutes, Junior watches him fight the blossoming flames as the black horn of feathers twists overhead. A heroic sight—at least, until, without warning, his father begins his descent before his smoking foe is properly extinguished. His boots slip on the rungs, then struggle to find them. Slip again. His hands slipping and catching, too. His face: wet, terrified—like Junior has seen him in his mind so many times before.

"Everything okay?" Junior says. It isn't. For a moment, after reaching the ground, his father refuses to answer. Can't seem to. Instead, he just stands there, pinching his nose, rubbing his face.

Closing his smoke-reddened eyes while panting. Trying and failing to steady whatever has been knocked off balance inside his head as the hose snakes water across their toes.

"The hose. Get the hose," his father finally says, a little slur to the words, a voice Junior has never heard before: "The barn, the barn. The barn . . ."

With the hose, Junior begins climbing toward where his father had just come from, into the black and flaming sky. He climbs for thirty seconds or twenty minutes—he can't be certain. Then he cranes his body over the roof, compressing the hose with his thumb and aiming the hissing stream at the flames until the smoking stops, despite every molecule of his body telling him to come back down—to flee and never return—until he hears his father say, "It's all right! You can come down now!"

Then Junior descends to the fresh lawn where he struggles to catch his breath. "Are you sure?" he manages to say. And his father smiles, not a face-buster but close. His best attempt—as if to mask this hidden pain Junior sees.

"Don't you think we should go to the hospital? You were slurring," he says. "You almost fell over, dad."

But, no, his father doesn't think they need to do that. He'll be all right. Just feels a little tired now. Nothing Junior needs to concern himself with. Nothing to tell his mother about. He used to play a doctor on TV, right? "Just lookit," he says with a thin laugh. There's still some furniture to throw into the pile. A fire to tend. Can Junior monitor the flames for him for a little, while he sits a spell in his truck? C'mon, it'll be fun to be in charge for once.

When Junior nods at this, his father tousles his hair. He side-hugs him before disappearing into the air-conditioning of his truck, leaving Junior standing there with the distinct feeling he's been taught something valuable, but not knowing what.

Next day, the vultures are gone, just like that: a wispy cloud where their black horn once spun. A bright white sun. From the bed of his truck, his father pulls a long, black box. "A casket?" Junior says.

"The hell's the matter with you," he says, unlocking the box: "It's your new friend."

Turns out, he'd rented a jackhammer to carve out that window hole in the stone foundation. The kitchen, remember? His mother was right, he'd decided: It was a hovel in need of light. He explains this like it warrants celebration, even more than a trip to the dump.

Then his father runs an extension cord outside, plugs it in, and the jackhammer kicks into life. He presses the chugging jackhammer into the foundation and sends a few crags of concrete flying. "Here," he says. "Now you try."

After two days of noise and dust, a small square of light appears in the foundation, first, falling upon the countertop, then the stone floors. Deeper and deeper, it soaks up the darkness, until the kitchen is sufficiently lighted.

The vibrations from the jackhammer echo inside Junior's hands and arms—a hot Styrofoam feeling that lasts for days, weeks. A melody that hums in his hands, then begins dissipating along with his fear of tragedy, all of it either compacted into garbage cubes or hidden beneath primer and paint now. Exploded with a lawn mower blade. Fading out of sight, forgotten through the familiarity of repetition. Turned to ash. Gone.

By spring, the farmhouse is ready to rent, and does so quickly, just like his father said, to an accountant, a single mother and her two children. Then, a few months later, to a firefighter. There's a web designer a few more months after that.

And it goes on like this. For months, a year. Two years. Junior is fifteen now and keeping tabs on the property for his father. Sixteen. The tenants breath their lives in and out of the walls, never staying long, moving on with the next steps in their lives.

"This business capitalizes on destruction and repair," his father explains, more than once, with a wink almost every time. "It's foolproof," he says. "Forget what your mother will tell you: My only regret is that I didn't leave Hollywood and start sooner. Didn't listen to my father. If I had started when I was your age, I would be filthy rich by now."

All through the rest of high school, Junior works there. He mows the lawn and bites lemons. Not with a scythe now, but with a new push mower his father buys. "Why did you ever make me use that awful scythe in the first place?" Junior asks him one day.

"I needed to teach you," his father says.

"Teach me what?"

"Hard work. Or rather the effect hard work brings you. The readiness and security. If you don't understand, you will, once you have your own family." The point is, the farmhouse isn't unpleasant anymore. Junior likes working there, feels like he understands more of why his father does what he does. The comfort in the idea of resurrection. The work even came with a view.

Without the anxiety roiling his gut, he finds the black dirt quite beautiful. The onions that bubble up to be collected by the migrants in bulging bags. George's house across the road and the silhouette it strikes at dusk. The single-wide trailers beyond that. The swollen and verdant valley wall. The swaths of clear blue skies above.

Whenever George drives by, Junior still waves to him. Sometimes, George stops and offers lemons. Pulls his oxygen mask to the side to talk about his myriad health problems, about his own madness. Still sharp in his own way, Junior supposes.

"Did he always look that bad?" his father says after observing this one day.

"Like an old, sick man?" Junior says. "As far as I can tell."

"He looks like death," Vic says—a comment that gives Junior pause. Ever since the barn nearly burned, he's noticed his father's attempts to cover up these blind spots. What he might've forgotten. After the stroke he reported having during the fire, he refused to see a doctor: "There's nothing they can do for me anyway," he said. "They'll just say, 'You may die.' I know that already. Plus, it'd only worry your mother."

To make him feel better, Junior admits he also forgets these kinds of details all the time: names, numbers, people's faces. Things he promised himself he'd remember. He searches for them in his mind but discovers only the void, an empty spot. "And I'm *only* sixteen," he says.

In fact, to stay sharp for them both, he now keeps a small notebook in his back pocket. On which, he writes down his father's to-do lists—the materials needed, the tasks ahead: *mow lawn, fix toilet, clean gutters, shovel dirt,* and so on. "Lookit," he says, and shows his father.

Today, his notepad reads, *Figure out what's going on across the road.*

The last time he'd been at the farmhouse, he'd noticed another truck parked next to George's. That the lawn was shabbier than usual, with a few free-range chickens he'd never noticed before roaming the lawn. So he decides to cross over there, knowing his father wouldn't appreciate this. The idea of these chickens' acidic shit ruining his lawn might raise his blood pressure to vein-bursting heights.

The solution was easy: Politely suggest they coop the chickens. Problem solved.

So Junior knocks on George's door. He knocks some more. He stands there on the sagging porch, waiting and running over just how he'll put it to the old man. But instead of George, a young man answers, wearing George's signature alligator-skin hat.

George's nephew, he's informed. "My uncle died nearly three months ago," the nephew says, a plug of tobacco in his lip. "Who'd you say you were again?" He spits past Junior into the high grass of what had been George's manicured yard.

What then ensues about the chickens doesn't go well—a conversation whose aftermath Junior later writes down in his notebook. "Shoot those chickens with a pellet gun. Shoot the man in his ass if he ever comes unwanted onto his father's property. Call the county to get after him about mowing that unruly lawn. Keep my father's brain from exploding."

In the weeks that follow, the conversation only turns grimmer. His father doesn't care about the chickens anymore. Never even broaches the subject at all. Never at dinnertime or driving somewhere in the truck—like you'd expect him to. He just wants to move in the new tenants. (This isn't his only property, after all.) Meanwhile, the nephew seems set on letting his chickens multiply out of spite and rage. On letting his grass grow long as the first time Junior ever set eyes on his father's farmhouse.

The new lawyer couple is already calling to complain about the chickens, the noise. Junior asks his father what he plans to do, readies himself to scribe down his father's orders in the notebook. But his father recommends no course of action.

"He's dangerous," Junior reminds him. "This nephew's capable of anything."

"Trust me. Just wait," is all his father says, and so that's that. And for a while, things do settle down. For too long. The lawyer couple either gets used to the unsightly grass and chickens roaming their yard or gives up caring about it—regardless, they don't move out. The rent keeps showing up. The machine his parents build still grinds on. As life resumes a type of rhythm—more foreclosed houses, more belongings, more trips to the dump, and burning trash. More erasure of people's lives. Until, wait, no, the lawyer couple decides to move out. Overnight, it seems, they've had enough. One day, just like that, they're gone.

His father doesn't flinch. He runs an ad in the newspaper: quaint farmhouse for rent. $1,800.

Meanwhile, Junior keeps waiting. But for what? While he works, he wonders, because the work asks you to wonder—whenever his father isn't around, he's heard his mother say as much. But when one subject remains for too long, what can you do? The joints go brittle. The energy saps. Whatever you do, you can't seem to crane your neck long enough to see around the question's mass. *What do you do to cope, then?* Junior writes. Between the lists he makes for his father, he likes to work through the possibilities of outcomes. To pose what-ifs, then color in what might happen. To cope, but also to make things happen. You can make anything happen. In bed at night, drifting into dreams, the cords in his upper arms tighten while his hand plays out these futures in a solid block of text.

His mother buys him notebooks and slips them to him like illicit drugs. He fills them up within days sometimes, about this and that—with stories that begin to rewrite themselves as soon as they end.

For instance, this is one version of how the story of the vulture
house ends:

*Owing to the nephew's curt nods, Junior knows he hasn't
forgotten their conversations. A woman lives with him now.
This cow with teeth he can tell are crooked from across the
road. Meanwhile, the rich black dirt sends the unmown grass
higher and higher, until it reaches up past the railings of their
porch, cropping up into their windows. The grass going to
seed. Doubling, tripling in thickness. Halfway up the house
almost. A fertility that, over time, seems to extend itself to the
girlfriend's swollen belly. Junior smiles, waves at her while he
mows. Meanwhile, the nephew's cigarette pulses like that
ember that almost burned down the barn those years ago.
The ember he put out and nearly killed his father with. But he
tries not to worry. He whittles away his anxiety by sharpening
his blade of exhaustion. He bites down on his own slice of
lemon. Works without tears, unafraid of what the future
holds. They'd never had trouble renting the farmhouse before.
At night, he sleeps like he's dead. Yet it's harder than they
expect to fill the old farmhouse after the lawyer couple left.
"You know what I'm going to say," his father says, and keeps
saying what he's been saying, to just wait, without actually
stating the idea that seems to hang off the edge of the phrase.
Did he lose a piece of his mind that day in the barn fire? Junior
wonders. Had he forgotten the omen, or had the omen gone
away? Like the vultures had disappeared with the part of him
that had been taken. But then, one day, Junior spies the vultures
again. Two, three. Four. Billowing their return over the valley's
rim. Like so many embers. Riding a current. The shape of
their wide wings coasting like his father's dented smile that*

day before the rotted barn. They aren't so evil now. After he'd assumed a man had been kicked out by his life, sequestered to spend his final days in squalor. The joy he'd found in that. But the family never died, Junior reminds himself. The degradation of a family, he thinks instead, as if it was something else to add to his notebook. (The notebook inside the story inside his notebook now.) Another tenant comes and goes. And Junior's back mowing the lawn again. In the black dirt, the grass grows higher and higher, it seems, with each passing season. Junior smiling and waving—almost seventeen now—as he circumnavigates the lawn in shrinking circles. Around and around. Until the sun goes down and the migrant trailer's lights come on. And the vultures gather, spinning heavy and slow overhead. A tornado of wings pulling the earth upward under their talons. Breathing in the world like a single lung. As new tenants become old tenants. And Junior's lists elongate in his mind as he mows, to remember more of what they'll need to do. Paint kitchen, clean bathroom, mow lawn, mulch garden. Burn remnants of discarded belongings. Relentlessly, Junior mows the lawn to keep the grass from getting out of hand. No shotgun shells to bend the blade to worry about anymore. No beer cans. He cuts swaths through the grass for the next tenants, bites down on another lemon. Used to this now. As the citrus burns a blister on his lip he didn't know he had. And he looks at the nephew and, through the yellow rind, begins humming—a song whose source, for the life of him, he can't remember. But if he looked, he's certain he'd find somewhere in his mess of notebooks, written down.

Junior Greener's eight-foot foam surfboard makes for a cumbersome walk along the one-lane dirt road toward the beach. Whenever a breeze kicks up, the surfboard bucks like a rogue sail, threatening to fly off into the dense elephant grass beyond. Between gusts he holds out a thumb for the parade of diesel-fueled Jeeps. Lashed with surfboards, they continue to pass him with the faint whiff of French fries. No one offers him a ride.

"Ohmmmmmmmmmm . . ."

Really, what did it matter? His two childhood friends (who shall not be named) flew home that morning. And the taxi wouldn't arrive at the hotel for another few hours to shuttle him to the sea turtle nesting ground in Ostional: the sight he'd spent the week trying and failing to convince them to go see. Until the trip had built into this imperative pilgrimage in his mind.

When Junior reaches the trailhead—this dark mouth through the palm trees no wider than his shoulders—another breeze kicks up. Stronger now. Wresting the surfboard from his hands. Sending it swirling off into the tall, swishing grass. He wades in after it, picks up the surfboard. Begins inspecting its smooth foam surface for dents and scratches. The grass whispers about his knees as his fingers glide over chunks of Sex Wax.

Then there's this rustling sound.

Junior cranes his neck wildly, expecting Costa Rica's deadliest snake—the deadly fer-de-lance, his father continually warned him about, as if he lacked the sense to not pick one up without his guidance—to rear its head when he least expected.

Instead, Junior discovers himself surrounded by these orange and blue crabs. Hundreds of them. Maybe thousands. Scuttling like flames out of pockets along the jungle floor. Had his two childhood friends drowned their sound out with their belligerence and roughhousing and mocking Tarzan calls? He suspects so, and much worse.

The first steps through the grass back to the road are near impossible—like lifting a concrete boot from a sucking bog—but get easier as he makes his way down the trail toward the beach. Then, all at once, the jungle falls away in rags. And he steps out into the sand, the ocean sprawling before him like a panorama of heaven.

All week, his two childhood friends had made it impossible for him to take it all in. Now, without them, the beach is an entirely different experience—the ocean no longer two parts hydrogen, one part oxygen, but an endless vat of liquid, shimmering diamonds. The sand: baby powder between his toes. The crashing waves: a poem, a lullaby. A visage that contained enough inspiration to fuel every story he's destined to write.

"Ohmmmmmmmmmmm . . ."

Really, Junior knows, he should be grateful for the mirror his friends hold up. For the way they'd made him cringe all week by opting for hamburgers instead of fresh-caught fish. How they'd pronounced English words in Spanish accents as if this would foster understanding, and pestered the bartender at the discoteca to score them a bag of Columbian white. Without them, he might not have decided to stay. Might've balked and returned home and resumed working for his father every day for the rest of his life.

Thank God! Because for Junior, it's only ever been his father's orders. His father's constant lessons on carpentry, on plumbing, on electric. Diatribes on building inspectors and regulations.

Workdays that span twelve, fourteen hours. Only ever dirty fingernails, paint-flecked clothes, boogers filled with spackle dust and insulation. The same gas station turkey sandwiches and burnt black coffee in a Styrofoam cup. The same bullfrogging of beer farts in the Lowe's bathroom and swarming yellowjackets teeming from gutters. Dilapidated soffits. Scales of lead paint. Houses full of the dead's stuff—

It's never been a freewheeling adventure for Junior. No—never his mother's youth. Never like the Tucson and Memphis and New Orleans she spoke of. The Montreal. The weightless drifting that he still senses in her now, that kept her forever idling, no matter the circumstance, at a level of joyous calm. Never Hollywood, California—the unsquarable intersection of his parents meeting. Where they'd conceived him without a house to their name in a rented apartment, while another, freer person—not his father—pursued an artistic career in the face of total financial ruin.

And after being exposed to paradise, what sane person would want to return to that life? Who wouldn't want to forge their own life, like those baby sea turtles? To unburden oneself of the rocks one's family stuffs in your pockets and float freely with the tide of one's own mind and interests? Creativity is the residue of rest, is it not?

Now Junior begins stretching. Like the other surfers around here do before paddling out. Instead of attempting yoga poses, however, he completes a battery of exercises he learned during his one season of JV football: toe touches, butt kicks, cherry pickers, so on. He pulls his leg up by the ankle, stretching his quad. The lineup bobs beyond the break. And he shields his eyes as one surfer glides across the horizon. Gut jumping as he notes the guy's foot position and stance, the way he leaned into the wave, skimming the glassy water with a single fingertip.

Soon, I will feel that, Junior thinks. Soon, I will be just as bearded and muscled and tan—my eyes filled with an ancient, patient wisdom, and words will flow unimpeded through my hand. "I'm going to pull a Robinson Crusoe," he told his friends before they left for Liberia airport that morning over plantains, eggs, and black coffee. But they'd been too busy complaining about the size of the coffee cups to take him seriously. "They're like thimbles," they said. And only later, after they loaded into the taxi, did they think to ask, "Where's your luggage, man?"

"I told you already," Junior said. "I'm leaving everything behind to become a novelist."

"Is this because we don't want to see those stupid sea turtles?" one friend said.

"Just get in the taxi, or we'll miss our flight," said the other.

Yet Junior hadn't budged. Instead, he simply lifted his arms, motioned toward the billowing jungle and uncapped skies beyond them. A fat parrot preened in a nearby palm, its fronds rocking gently in the sweet breeze. "Don't cause a scene," his friend said.

Am I causing a scene? Junior wondered. The taxi driver didn't seem overly concerned. Nor did the bag boy. Even the mermaid fountain was spitting water in a highly agreeable manner. "Listen," he said. "Tell my parents sorry, tell my father—"

"Tell him yourself," his other friends said, before climbing into the taxi. "It's your funeral."

Of course, Junior had never surfed a day in his life. But in bearing witness to one effortless display after the other from the beach, he was filled with an undeniable confidence, and unable to contain himself any longer, he thrusts his surfboard like a spear and charges at the water. Leaping headlong into the surf, where he coasts out across the water with a grace that surpasses even his own expectations. And as his toes drag through the warm water and the salt pleasantly burns away the itch from a week's worth of mosquito bites and sunburns, he's struck with a vision of himself. So vivid and pure. He feels as if he's molted from his past self, his exoskeleton abandoned in the sand. Now his better self has been reborn in the crashing waves, swimming through the deep ocean of his future.

In a year's time, he'd forge himself a modest shack of corrugated tin. And in the fertile soil behind the shack, he'd grow vegetables, coffee beans. Each night, after a delicious and healthy dinner, he'd feed the collarless dogs and blue-and-orange crabs his leftovers before spending his night at his typewriter. Instead of wealth, the acquisition of properties and endless workdays, he'd crave nothing more than the crash of the distant surf, the twinkle of stars. The call-and-response of the howler monkeys chugging high up in the trees. The book deal to come.

This grace doesn't last long, however. The first wave swells, crests, crashes. Then, like some schoolyard bully, shoves Junior down, as, for a few elongated seconds, he's dragged along in a salty spin cycle that mashes him repeatedly against the sandy ocean floor. Holds him there. For too long. Far too long. Moments before his lungs seize, the wave spits him out about twenty yards closer to shore. Sputtering. Sinuses abuzz with saltwater. His shoulder aching from sand scrub.

And yet—for as broken as his body feels, his spirits are not. This is just how Robinson Crusoe began his journey, Junior thinks, before climbing back atop his surfboard and beginning to paddle out again.

Upstate New York. Vic paces the rank and cluttered darkness of this vinyl bi-level he and Heather just purchased at the county auction for a prayer. Out near Pine Island, with a nice view of the onion fields. A sort of graduation present he'd convinced her to buy for their son, that they'd gift him the moment he returned home.

Or maybe not a present exactly, Vic thinks. Something better. An opportunity. To make some real money. Go partners with his old man. Like he always regretted not doing with his own father after the reality check of a wife and child. For Junior to start his path of success that much sooner. To help his future self. In ten years, he could have his own machine of passive income. Then he could sit back and write his novels, if that's what he still wanted.

Out the windows, the onion fields sprawl, miles of bubbling black ocean as the beam of his flashlight illuminates snatches of countertops strewn with broken plates, walls covered in obscene graffiti. A toilet with a drowned rat bloating inside. Meanwhile, his head brushes through these cobwebs and gusts of eerie cold make his breath briefly smoke.

Already, there's a positive feeling here for Vic. Forget the good bones, the solid plumbing. Forget the relatively new fuel-oil tank sitting in the garage. There's a solid foundation here for his son to build from. For him to help build with his son. Already, he can imagine the finished product—the amount of money the renovated bi-level would fetch, the hunger the success would inspire for the next foreclosure. And the one after that.

While Vic paces, every now and then, he stops, trains the flashlight on the small Moleskine notebook he borrowed from his son's stack to scribble down another note on the materials they would need to get started. Another utility provider. Another contractor he'd need to call. *Garbage bags, trailer,* he writes. *Five-gallons of spackle, tape, Kilz oil-primer. Call Orange and*

Rockland. The list grows, grows. Grows. The preparations truly endless.

I'll have to stop at Home Depot, he thinks. I'll have to spend the rest of the night making calls. Get everything ready. If he didn't get home late, if the traffic from JFK wasn't that bad, perhaps, Junior would want to start as soon as tomorrow morning.

Push broom, Windex, paper towels, dust masks, he writes.

The taxi to Ostional is late. The concierge keeps telling Junior, "Soon, soon." But he's getting antsy, has already drank a couple of Imperials and sips a third. Perched on a wicker barstool, he scratches the sunburned mosquito bites on his body, peers through the marble archway toward the roundabout where the taxi scuttled off with his two childhood friends that morning. It feels like weeks ago.

"Ohmmmmmmmmmm . . ."

Is there time to order a quick meal? He decides against it. In the lobby, there's a computer with internet access that keeps drawing his eyes. While he waits, he hates the urge he feels to log on. Yet in five minutes time, he finds himself doing just that and opening his email. The corners of his mouth creep upward while his fingers clatter. Through the buffer of so many hundreds of miles, he soon finds, he can express himself freely, say the things to his father that he's always wanted.

When the taxi arrives, he stops writing the email midsentence, hits send, vanishing the endless block of text he's amassed these twenty minutes into the void. Then he finishes his Imperial in a single pull and jogs across the lobby, out the marble archway, and climbs in up front with the Tico driver: a man with a shiny bald head, a Coca-Cola T-shirt, a silver stud in one ear. "Ostional?" he says.

Soon, through the passenger-side window, Junior recognizes nothing. Along the coast, even the fauna seems different. Bigger with sharper edges. The shadows the jungle held: that much darker. Full of mystery. Due to the minefield of potholes, the driver can push the diesel-fueled Jeep no faster than fifteen miles an hour. But even at this speed, Junior remains exhilarated with the prospect of starting over here. Maybe he'd practice his Spanish enough to become fluent in a year. "¿Que pasa?" he says. "¿Bueno?"

To which, the driver answers, at length and far too quickly. Just this jumble of incoherence to his ears from which he catches only fragments: "Cansado . . . distancia . . . llegar tarde . . ."

"¿Que? Hablar mas slowly," Junior says.

The driver tries again, slower, but still too fast. Making clear that Junior didn't understand enough to hold a genuine conversation. "I'm going to check out the sea turtle nesting grounds," he says, giving up and switching over to English. "Those prehistoric leatherbacks?"

But the driver seems to know just about as much English as Junior knows Spanish, and the process is repeated in reverse. Soon, their conversation dwindles into silence, and his mind turns back toward his empty inbox.

While he knows the news of his expatriation probably hasn't yet reached his father, he still wishes he could check his email on his cell phone. He has no idea what to expect regarding a reaction. But the more he thinks about it, the more Junior finds himself hoping for an irrevocable cutting of cords. The impossibility of turning back, leaving him with no one to help him dig his way from his nest and crawl into the rainforest, where he'd build his shack. Like the storm that'd sent Robinson Crusoe on his path toward inner peace and harmony. His mother would understand.

It takes over an hour to reach signs of the town. Then Ostional— or at least the beginnings of what might become Ostional—begins presenting itself in a slow trickle of corrugated tin shacks, chicken wire, small fields and pastures. Grazing Brahman cows. A few stucco houses surrounded with barbed wire that swell and fade from the road like a tide.

Junior keeps waiting for the telltale signs of the church and soccer field that characterize every other larger town they've passed through until now. But the driver simply pulls over, stops, seemingly at random. "¿Bueno?" he says.

"¿Bueno?" says Junior. "¿Donde?"

"Ostional."

"Ostional?" Looking up and down the thin dirt road, Junior searches for signs or arrows. A roving group of tourists he could follow to where he wanted to go. But like the church/soccer field combo, there are no telltale markers to guide him. "The sea turtles are here?" he says, making little digging motions with his hands.

"The sea turtles, *yes*," the driver says. "Just over there," he says, without pointing.

Now Junior opens the taxi's door, steps out. Having spent the entire week trying to coax his two childhood friends here, to see this sublime and inspirational sight—even one night going so far as to hide their cocaine and hold it ransom while hysterically repeating he was doing this for their own good, even crying a little, until they agreed to consider the idea—what other choice did he have?

When the driver rolls down the window, he hands him the last of his *colones*, which the driver accepts without making change.

"Gracias. Pura vida," he says, and drives off before Junior can ask him where to go or for a phone number to reach him for a ride back.

Without any real direction, Junior begins walking. His bare feet slap the warm dirt as something crashes through the trees high above him, while, further off in the distance, an animal—maybe a bird—trills violently.

"Ohmmmmmmmmmm . . ."

A diesel truck passes, kicks up another cloud of dust, through which several sullen-faced Ticos stare back at him from the bed of the truck. There's that same whiff of French fries. Junior works the collar of his shirt up over his mouth against the dust, keeps walking, eventually coming to a matted swath of yellow grass running between two barbed-wired houses, a sort of trail that he ducks down with speedy hesitance. Somewhere in the distance a dog barks.

Now the palm trees slam up to form a dark tunnel around him. The legions of blue-and-orange crabs resume their rustling. Tens of thousands now, maybe more, making each of his steps more difficult—a concrete boot in a sucking bog.

Nevertheless, like those sea turtle hatchlings toward the waves, Junior wills himself down the darkening trail. One step after the other, after the next. Until, all at once, the trees fall away, and he bears witness to the sand, the ocean. That same heavenly panorama. But after glancing up and down the beach, Junior sees no sea turtles. No eggs or hatchlings. No people. No signs. This beach, it's as desolate as the town.

He watches the golden beams of the setting sun play on the frothy lips of the cresting waves. There are no surfers here. He looks up and down the beach, squinting his eyes. Until eventually, there, in the distance: a speck of motion. A piece of driftwood or a roaming collarless dog? Without any other viable options, he starts toward it, hoping for the speck to clarify into a mob of people. Which it does. Into at least thirty, forty Ticos. Maybe more. Men, women, children. Old, young. The entire town. The sea turtle nesting ground!

Thank God, Junior thinks, and keeps walking toward the signs of the sublime sight he'd anticipated all week already evident now: The beach here appears raked by great tines, the sand piled haphazardly in sloping dunes where the sea turtles must've dug. The holes where the hatchlings will launch their lives.

Craning his neck, he hopes to spy one seventy-five-pounder like he'd read about—a female laying a clutch of eggs—but the crowd is too dense. Many of the Ticos are crouched in the sand, scooping at the earth with their arms, the surf nearly kissing their toes. "Excuse me," Junior says, trying to catch a glimpse. "Excuse me, please! Por favor—"

Something rolls past him. Down the beach through the damp sand. After which a mutant-looking dog lopes in pursuit. Bare patches of skin alternating with dreadlocks of gray fur over his body. His protruding teeth make a clicking sound, like an engine turning over as his feet fling sand. Until at last there is an explosion in the sand.

Strings of yolk hang from this dog's scraggly chin as he trots proudly back up the beach toward an older Tico woman with cropped hair in a T-shirt with a palm leaf crest emblazoned on its breast pocket. The woman removes another egg from a five-gallon bucket, which reminds Junior of the buckets his father used to clean paint brushes. Briefly, she appraises it, then cocks her arm again, throws.

"No wait—" Junior says.

But, already, the dog and the sea turtle egg go whizzing by his feet. The older Tico woman regards him with a neutral expression, says something in Spanish. Then, after registering his confusion, she points at herself.

"For us, not you," she says.

Junior has no idea what she's talking about. Even if he spoke Spanish fluidly, he had a feeling understanding was an entire continent away: "Ohmmmmmmmmmm. . . ." But it's useless now. His brain's been reduced to a kernel on the brink of combustion.

"I'm sorry, so sorry," he says. "No comprende." Now he begins backing away, apologizing and holding up his quaking palms, continuing to do so long after the Tico woman rejoins the others and resumes shoveling sea turtle eggs into her five-gallon bucket in the dying light. "Lo siento," he remembers, suddenly, and starts repeating this as well. Backing away still. "Lo siento, lo siento . . ." Until his naked heel brushes something beneath the choppy wet sand, and his *lo sientos* stop.

Very slowly, Junior crouches down, grinds his knees into the cool, firm sand. Where he begins carving out the edges of something in the sand around the egg his foot had touched, a prize which he now carefully extracts and tucks, cold and clotted with sand, under his unbuttoned shirt. Before creeping down the beach like some sort of PETA secret operative, his heart chainsawing away inside his bare and sunburnt chest.

The sun executes its final roll over the horizon, plunging the entire scene into night in a span of time that seems to take three breaths. The sheen along the eggshell fades in his trembling hands.

And so, as the Ticos begin streaming off the beach, arms straining with loaded five-gallon buckets, Junior decides to follow them at a careful distance, stumbling and sluicing through the sand, suddenly hungry for the hot meal he'd forgone back at the resort, another Imperial. But as the group of Ticos quickly thins, drifts off in separate directions, he soon finds himself alone again.

"Ohmmmmmmmmm . . ."

The mantra proves useless, though, as he surveys the darkened ridges of sand before him, slowly being eaten up by the tide. And after stumbling through what may or may not have been a trail, he returns to the dirt road he'd been dropped off on earlier, where he discovers a wooden bench that might be a bus stop. He sits, holds the egg against himself and tries to decide the best way to get home. His cell phone displays no bars.

Darkness soon weighs on him. There are no stars tonight. Thick rain clouds have rolled in, as if to form total night. Through which, he can hear nothing but the soft tossing of ocean waves, the insects and monkeys awakening in the walls of trees that surround him.

Minutes pass, maybe an hour of staring into the heavy blackness, trying to figure out how to proceed, how to help himself. Until he sees the flicker of a small red light, or thinks he does, anyway. A Coca-Cola sign, perhaps?

Half-blind, he jogs toward it, the noise of the jungle rising again. A cacophony of breaking branches, swishing grass, slithering snakes. More scuttling crabs. Split-tongued monsters. And so many more dangers he doesn't care to meet or understand.

His stomach gurgles louder now. With each hurried step, he thinks of nothing but the prospect of a meal, a phone call. Another Imperial. His bed. The egg slipping against his sweat-slick skin as his shirt cracks like a cape through the pitch-dark night.

Around ten o'clock, Eastern Standard Time, Vic's preparing to call it a night. He's been at his desk, pushing bills around and making phone calls to contractors for the past few hours. Completing the ceremony of setting up what needs setting up for the return of his new partner, his son. All the materials from the lists that morning have already been purchased, are waiting for them in the bed of his truck.

He doesn't keep a clock in his office, but realizes it's quitting time by the ache in his bones and eyes. Now it's time to migrate downstairs into his kitchen, pour himself two fingers of tequila. Catch up on his TV shows with his lovely wife. Or maybe she'd be up for a roll?

However, tonight, for whatever reason, after shoving his rolling chair away from the desk, Vic decides to check his email one last time. There's nothing too pressing. Nothing that couldn't wait until the morning, really. But there's something nagging him in his gut. So, he scoots back to the keyboard and logs on. Refreshes his inbox, and *I'll be damned*—a message from his son.

After reading a few lines of what appears to be an endless email, Vic leans back in his chair, begins rubbing his face and eyes. *I hereby renounce all ties to the Greener lineage*, a line reads. *Never again will I benefit from the foreclosure of a home*, reads another. He rereads the text, trying to will himself to doubt its authenticity, the strange formality of the language. This pidgin legalese. The literary flourishes. But the rubbing and the attempts to will the words away prove fruitless. These words came from his son.

Vic reads a couple more lines, hoping now that his son might come to his senses (he isn't a stupid boy, just impulsive, easily influenced). But no. The boy's deathly serious. *If only he'd said these things before*, he thinks. In his presence. He, they, could've done better for him. Could've prevented him from making the mistakes he had. Vic would've placed that right there at the top of his list: *Help my son feel more like his own man.* At least enough to not feel the need to make this false start. To pursue his creative life without burning his future down.

Jesus Christ. Holy hell. My God—

Then the landline rings, and Vic's so immersed in the email, he actually jumps up, discovers himself standing bolt-upright. Surprised to find himself inside his own body, in his own home. His office with the raccoon photograph hanging over the peephole in the wall. Where he's been all night. With this block of text still glaring at him. His son, so far off. Is it even possible? The phone rings again.

Rings.

Rings—

Finally, Vic picks up. "Son?" But it's only this robotic voice, mumbling something then erupting into static. So loud, he almost hangs up, believing the call to be just another telemarketer, a mistaken credit shark. One of the countless real estate agents that pester him like the plague with new house-flipping projects. But then he hears something else. Through the static, inside it: a voice.

"Please accept a collect call from . . ." the voice says, accompanied by a certain nervous desperation. And it comes to him in a flash—what's happened, is happening now: Not two paragraphs into Vic reading his email declaring independence, his son is calling collect to take back everything he said. To apologize to his old man. Beg to remain partners.

Our smart boy! Vic thinks and swivels toward the window. Outside, a full moon sits behind a leafless tree. *"Please accept a collect call from . . ."* the robot repeats. Then comes blasts of the voice again, shrill and glorious—his son's.

Vic listens, smiles. Outside the branches rattle in the cold breeze, a blob of shadow perched in one of them. A bird of some kind, he realizes. Perhaps the owl that sometimes peers at him while he works. The wise bird! Whatever it is, the animal senses his attention and flaps its wings, sailing off into the night. Off to find a mouse, to drop a pellet, to feed its child, Vic isn't certain. But either way, it's a miraculous sight.

THE GROTTO

Out of the blue, West Shapiro calls—an old buddy from Vic Greener's acting days. Who played the arresting officer of his character: Dr. Mack on the long-running soap opera *Days of our Lives*. Turns out, he's just gotten remarried to a woman half his age, moved to a suburb in North Jersey, and hopes the Greeners can attend their housewarming party.

Heather wants to go. Or, rather, wants Vic to want to go. But Vic has no interest. What did she think they were going to do? Drink tequila, snort cocaine, and hit the Chateau Marmont? "There's too much to do around here, anyway," he says.

"That's ridiculous," Heather says. With eight rental properties, there will always be something to do around here. Money to collect! An apartment to show! A leaky faucet to fix! And so, does that mean Vic doesn't plan to have another experience outside of maintaining these degrading old houses for the rest of his life? "C'mon. I want to have some old-fashioned fun," she says.

So, that weekend, Vic yields. They drive down to North Jersey—or *America's armpit* as he continually refers to the dense traffic and crammed-in houses that roll through the windows of his truck while he drives. "Who'd want to live in such a place?"

"Hon, the road?" Heather smooths the blue hem of her dress—this low-cut, sheer throwback outfit Vic had somehow forgotten.

A dress he now remembers West Shapiro picking off a rack at a thrift store in Santa Monica another lifetime ago. How Vic had thought they'd been searching for *his* gift. But then, at the register, West purchased the sexy number for Heather's birthday himself. An inappropriate gift to receive from a friend, no doubt. Then comes another memory of West later on: drunk on margaritas back at Vic's apartment at the Oakwood, making a big deal about his forgetting and leaving the price tag on. "Secrets out, then," he said.

Now Vic can't take his eyes off her.

"I'm serious," Heather says. "The road!"

Finally, a street differentiates itself with a bevy of sleek sedans and high-end luxury SUVs. At the end of which, Vic parks his truck. Through the dusty windshield, a gaudy colonial stands proudly, white-columned and groomed-hedged. Big black balloons billow off the mailbox. The lawn: freshly mown into healthy strips.

They start down a brick path toward the sounds of a party, along a mulchy garden peppered with perennials and birdbaths. Past a Japanese maple that has grown grafted into the chicken wire someone clearly wrapped around it years ago, as a sapling. Into a modest expanse of yard choked with terraced gardens, snaking brick paths, oversize faux-wicker patio furniture.

People are everywhere. More than Vic's seen together in person in years. Dozens of them holding champagne flutes in what appears to be designer garb. Servers in bowties ducking in and out serving shrimp puffs. The glowing blue pool with a waterfall shimmering like a dehydration victim's last kitsch mirage—

"Doctor Mack, *sir*!"

After all this time, Vic still recognizes the gruff honk of his friend's voice. West's appearance, however, as he turns, much less so. He's red-faced and puffy, a sunburnt dome of head like a crab's shell where his flowing black hair used to perch—a discrepancy that causes Vic to hesitate, however momentarily, leaving West to embrace Heather first. With a familiarity that hasn't dissipated, he lifts her squirming into the air.

Finally, he sets her down, only to begin tapping his chin and admiring her like a work of art: "Hey—I know that dress," he says, then drags her away by the arm, leaving Vic to follow them toward a white-linen-topped bar. Where, despite their protests, West proceeds to order from the bow-tied bartender: "Two margaritas with extra lime and salted rims." Their old drinks of choice—as Vic recalls—slosh at the rims as the bartender hands them over.

"C'mon," West says. "I won't rap out with either of you until you drink. Please. For the love of God. Drink!" And only then, after the prerequisite sips have been taken, does he turn to Vic and ask him what he's been up to.

Where to begin? Vic thinks, suddenly flushed. Moving back East? Heather's prolonged pregnancy? The buying and fixing up of what would become their house two decades ago? The buying and fixing up of so many more foreclosed houses? The parade of problem tenants they've dealt with? The fun they've had? The freakish garden Heather keeps in their backyard? How their son works for them now, hoping to learn the family business? Another link in the Greener chain?

Somehow, Vic manages through the more appetizing of these footnotes while catching glimmers of Heather sipping a margarita in that dress. Or at least tries the best he can—until West butts in, as if to save him from himself: "You always were handy," he says.

"I like to think so," Vic says, glancing at Heather as if he needs her to confirm this fact. As if, in the presence of West, the reality of his life has been brought into question. She, of course, nods on cue and sips at her margarita again.

West smiles over the lime wedged onto his glass. He snaps his fingers. "Hey, Vic, you know what—I was gonna ask you— there's this pesky water stain. Around the skylight in my bed- room. I've called every contractor in the county, but for whatever reason, the leak keeps coming back. Care to check it out for me?"

"I really don't know how much I could add," Vic says. "Did they check the window flashing? Any tears in the shingles? A downed branch?"

"I'm sure it'll be a piece of cake. Once you see it—"

Vic shields his eyes, points up at the tall, slanting, new roof of the three-story house. "I'd need a forty-foot ladder to see that. I'd need to tie off a rope for a harness. I'm not equipped for that, old buddy."

"I'll show you the damage inside, so you see what I mean. C'mon, you'd be really doing me a favor." But before Vic can respond—before he can say no way—West tells them to stick around. He'll be back as soon as he finds his wife to hang with Heather while they take care of that persistent leak. He has a forty-foot ladder, somewhere. In the guest house perhaps. "Do. Not. Move. A. Muscle," he says, and shuffles off into the crowd of champagne flutes with a wink.

Vic eats a shrimp puff. Heather eats a shrimp puff. Then, with their greasy shrimp puff napkins balled in their hands, they stand there watching the waterfall in the pool in silence instead of chatting between themselves or inanely with the other guests.

Five, ten minutes pass in this fashion. During which, they drink their drinks down to the lime wedges, but don't order another round. They eat more shrimp puffs. Vic wipes at the grease on his chin with the ball of already-greasy napkin. "What's with this guy?" he says, finally.

"What do you mean?" Heather says.

"Does he really think I'm going to climb a ladder in front of all these guests?"

"Of course not. He's always been a jokester," she says.

"I don't know," he says, and falls silent.

Once upon a time, it's true, Vic might've slipped his hand around Heather's waist, contented himself with the smooth feel of her hip beneath the fabric, made some joke, or conveyed some insider news meant to impress her. But the dress renders these actions inappropriate. Causes him to pluck his lime out of the glass and chew at its sourness without elaborating instead, while side-eyeing the thin straps of her dress, trying and failing to discern if she'd left the price tag on all these years.

At long last, West reemerges with a young woman. Elfish with auburn hair. Curvy in a silver sequin dress not too dissimilar from Heather's. Yet no doubt half their age. Faye—his second wife. This actress who starred in the soap years after both Vic and West's characters were written off. "The infamous Dr. Mack," West says.

"I think you might've killed my mother on the show," Faye says. "I think you might've illegitimately fathered my half-brother."

Vic smiles, trying to decide if she's kidding or not. "Who was your mother? Your half-brother?" he says.

However, his question goes unanswered. Or, rather, it's cannibalized by the cross-chatter of wives: Heather complimenting Faye's dress, her new home, and her new husband, saying what a catch he is. Faye insisting that no, no way, she should be the jealous one. Just look at Heather in that lovely *vintage* dress. Faye has heard everything about their good old days at the Oakwood, back in Hollywood.

"*Everything* everything!?" Heather says.

"Everything," Faye says with a knowing smile. "But that dress!" she says. "My God!"

Now West claps Vic on the shoulder. "What do you think about all this, good doctor? High time we dealt with that leak then?"

With a relenting nod, Vic allows West to ferry him through a pair of French doors—glad to escape the fake-smiled smooshing of the wives and their gestures toward a perplexing past—into an open concept living room/kitchen where he immediately recognizes a cheap, faux-granite countertop that reeks of IKEA and an equally tasteless white carpet that a person could never comfortably drink coffee or red wine on that stretches across the living room. Then, moving up a curving set of stairs and down a long hallway past a series of prints of framed paintings and photographs that even he recognizes:

Ansel Adams.

Picasso.

Monet.

The master bedroom opens like a bright cathedral. Completely unblemished around the skylight. The same tasteless artwork adorning the walls. The ceiling slanted and smooth. No water stains as far as he can tell.

"What's all this about?" Vic says, still searching.

Now West starts fishing in his pocket, removes a small mirror off the wall, places it on the four-post bed. Proceeds to use his wife's credit card to deftly break up the lines he pours there from a little baggie, forming a shape that's ridge-backed and ultra-white as the ceiling above. Just the sight of it sets Vic's nose dripping.

"Oh, no," Vic says.

"Oh, yes," West says and holds out that rolled-up dollar.

* * *

The pool is less kitsch now. The gardens less mulchy. The lines of West's home are more defined. While it's still gaudy, Vic must admit, perhaps he hadn't fully appreciated its design.

If a crane hoisted my old Victorian house to North Jersey, would it smack of pretension any less than this? he thinks. Reverse snobbery is what it was. It's all so obvious to him now—or, rather, the answers feel within reach, if he chose to articulate them.

Instead, he allows West to order another round of margaritas at the bar. Where they begin reminiscing about their days at the Oakwood together. The wives seem to have disappeared completely, which is more than fine with Vic. He feels himself opening up toward his friend like a sun-dappled flower. Stepping back into the good old days, he hears himself praising West for his courage:

"Pursuing a life in the arts is a constant battle," he says. "Against the terrible pressures of responsibility. This machine that, much like life, usually chews you up in the end. Eventually pulls you under, no matter how strong a swimmer you are. Even the best among them," he adds.

"Don't be ridiculous," West says. "I audition in New York now and then. But that's the extent of things, at the minute. I never had your talent."

"Me!?" Vic says. "I'm over here flipping foreclosed houses."

"You, indeed!" West says. "When you played the doctor, your own mother wouldn't have recognized you. If I had that kind of talent, I wouldn't be out here fighting for less-than-five-liners. Vying for my agent's attention. But sheesh: Heather? That's no small consolation, *am I right?*"

"You think so?"

"To see her in that dress again? I'd have done what you did in a heartbeat. I'd trade with you now."

Flooded with a newfound appreciation for his life, Vic plucks the lime from his glass and rips at the pulp with his teeth, chewing with all the power he imagines a pit bull might carry within its muscled jaws. He tosses the lime onto the pavers and flips the empty glass upside-down, half-expecting a bell to chime with glory. "Refill?" he says.

They start drifting around the party, neither eating shrimp puffs nor looking with any real concern for their wives, and instead, staring into each other's eyes without blinking and speed-talking, hardly believing that twenty years had passed.

If a partygoer approaches, West introduces Vic as "his fellow soap star, now successful renovator of foreclosed houses, with this knock-out of a wife." An old aspiring playwright, underwear model, spokesman, poet laureate of the Oakwood apartments, among other honorable titles. You name it. A lucky man by all measures. A Midas touch. "Hire him to act. Hire him to paint your house," he says more than once. "You won't be disappointed."

A while later, by the pool, they're still talking like this. They've taken off their shoes and are dipping their feet into the heated water that undulates before them with the super-tasteful waterfall's continuous crashing on the far end. As they take turns fishing the key to Vic's truck into West's baggie, Vic snorts and massages his sinuses. Thinks he spies a recess behind the curtain of water. A darkness with depth.

"Wait," he says. "Is that a grotto?"

"That's a grotto," West says, laughing.

"What's so funny?"

"Faye hated the idea. And even though it's mostly her family's money, I made such a big stink about having one. But, owing to the move and renovations, I still haven't been inside."

Vic feigns outrage at the thought of being too busy working on one's house to live in it. He says it's a high sin to neglect a grotto. And if he had a grotto, he'd pay said grotto its respect. He'd worship said grotto. He'd sacrifice small animals to said grotto. He'd drink fishbowls of tequila with his wife every night in that grotto and appreciate that grotto, his grotto, for every fucking grottoed thing it's worth.

"Don't be so certain," West says.

Then Vic begins unbuckling the belt holding up his trousers. After stripping down into his boxers, Vic slips into the water and wades toward the grotto, that dark sinus of faux rock, not really caring if West follows or not. The echoes of water slam up around him. The blue of the pool wobbles in the nooks of the low-hanging ceiling like ancient magic. An unclarified knowing springs into him from a previously untapped well, deep in his heart.

Then, suddenly, West bursts through the waterfall, shouting. His hands: formed into a finger gun. "Show yourself, Doctor Mack! I know you're in here!" he says in a voice that doubles off the water and ceiling and walls.

Even after all these years, it still amazes Vic how the lines from that final scene of his arrest returns to him. How the icy gaze reinstates itself in his eyes. "What makes you think I'm hiding, Officer Whitaker," he says, this sociopathic doctor.

Now West—or rather, Detective Whitaker—swings his finger gun, training the weapon on Dr. Mack, who, by all appearances, is unaffected by such threats. Icy as ever. He smiles back with the smile of a man with a bomb in his pocket not afraid to die. "Be careful where you point that."

"Just like you were careful with those drugs you sold my best friend's wife?" West says. "Just like how you were careful with that arsenic you used to lace her dose?"

Here, the frozen cast of Dr. Mack's face begins slipping—giving the would-be daytime audience their first glimpse of his apprehension over his impending death—before that affectless mask reinstates itself.

"Sticks and stones, Detective Whitaker," Vic says. "We both know your chief will have your badge if you arrest me."

Instinctively, Vic takes a step stage left while West moves stage right. Somehow, miraculously, both of them remember the scene's blocking. Somehow, they hit their marks with all of the harmony of the grotto's lights and sounds.

West keeps his finger gun trained at his happily racing heart. "You don't think I know that? You don't think I know you sell half of my police department drugs?" he says.

"Ah—vigilante justice, now, is it?"

Now a quake enters Detective Whitaker's finger gun. He makes to lower his service revolver, then raises it again with heightened resolve. His voice shakes off the grotto's shifting walls: "I love her, man. I would've done anything for her, man. My life could've been different. But you stole her. You took her away from me. Now she's ruined. She's as good as dead."

Vic pauses, snaps his fingers. But the next lines don't come, won't come.

"You took her away," West says, seemingly trying to prompt him. Eyes watering and quivering lips—a performance from him better than Vic can ever recall.

But, still, the line refuses Vic—or, at least, a line that jibes with what West's saying refuses him. Because, suddenly, the way he remembers it, the scene in his mind ended rather differently—with the detective bringing up fingerprint evidence instead of his best friend's wife. Evidence that meant he had him legally dead to rights.

Is he confusing the scene with another? It's possible. But wasn't the officer's best friend's wife the detective's sister? He doesn't remember incest being part of any plot. He's almost certain. Much too risky for daytime television back then.

Now the doctor's face melts into something far different.

"You stole the love of my life," West continues, his finger gun quivering again.

But still, nothing, the question of the next line still hanging there. And hanging there. Until, without any other option, Vic collapses into forced laughter, causing West to laugh too. The sound of them together swelling against the faux rock like madness. Laughing, laughing, laughing—this echo of laughter that continues long after Vic's had enough.

"Another toot, then?" West says after the sound dies off.

"I don't think so," Vic says. "I need to find my wife."

By the time they dry off and come back down to the party, Heather and Faye are standing at the bar. Waiting for them. Right where they initially left them. Like they'd never gone. They sip two large margaritas, chatting. Perhaps they're even the same drinks as before.

"Time to get going," Vic says, wrapping his comment in what could reasonably be construed as a question. And Heather looks at him and smiles a smile that communicates her understanding that something's soured for him here. That it's time to go. Right now.

She rakes a hand through his wet hair, smiles. "We do have a long drive back," she says, faking a yawn, stretching. Her dress is slightly off-kilter now, Vic notices. Her lips flushed. Like when she's drank too much or rubbed her fair skin against someone.

But how? he wonders, idiotically. *I've been with West this entire time.*

"Ready when you are," she continues, smiling brightly. Then again to her hosts, "We really do have a long drive back."

"But you've only just got here," West tells her. "How about another marg? Just one more. Your favorite. Our favorite!"

But Heather only smiles an apology at him. The women kiss cheeks. The men shake hands. West hugs Heather, his hands on her hips until Vic tugs her away by the arm. Then, while he pulls her away, Faye begins attempting to make tentative plans for next month, sometime, which, owing to the length of that hug, Vic knows will never come to pass.

"Great catching up. See you soon," he says, moving further off.

He leads Heather through the gate very quickly. Down the brick path, past the Japanese maple, to the end of the street. The truck. Her dress shedding shivers of light while they rush.

"Is that what you meant by some old-fashioned fun?" he says.

"You tell me," she says, giggling.

"I don't know," he says and removes the keys from his pocket. He jingles them at her to convey his resolve to drive even though he's been drinking. "I don't know anything, only that I'll be driving home tonight."

She doesn't argue with him, doesn't express any concern for their safety. Instead, she sparkles around to the side of the car and sits passenger and proceeds to fiddle with the radio while they drive along through the less-dense traffic, the same crammed-in houses.

Vic glances down at the speedometer, realizes he's speeding. Slows down, head swiveling with paranoia for cops. But when he looks down, he's speeding again. He sniffs a little after some cocaine crumbs.

After a few miles, Heather says that his upper lip is sweating. And a few more miles after that that, his cheeks are flush. Like they used to when he used to mix margaritas and fuck all night back at the Oakwood. Like when they used to go to that dive bar with the satin booths and mirrors on the ceiling off Rodeo Drive with West and whatever bimbo he wore on his arm.

"Remember that?" she says.

Of course, Vic does. In theory, anyway. Wind whips through the truck. And he focuses on this wind. He can't help it: the way the wind tornadoes her black hair in his peripheral vision. Teasing it higher and higher like how she once wore it. Back then, in the eighties—twenty, almost thirty years ago now? The price tag flaps its inordinate price at him, a number that's not so inordinate now.

He drives, thinking this and glancing at the speedometer every so often but still unable to stop speeding, wanting to return home and bury them in the comfort of their family life as soon as possible. Though now he's uncertain if Heather perceives this divide, has ever forgotten. Was he the sole forgetter? Had he been neglecting his grotto, too? Is that what West had meant?

His molars grind. "Where've you been?" he says.

"I've been here the entire time."

"No, did you sleep with him?" he says.

"With who?"

"With West," he says.

"You mean tonight?" Heather says, laughing.

"Is he even mine?"

And Heather keeps laughing. "You mean Junior?" she says.

The traffic is even thinner now. Nonexistent. A half hour, and already the terror of crammed-in houses has passed. As if dissolving into the steep grade of the Ramapo Mountains. Into the rising, slate-filled earth. "Don't be silly. It happened before we even started dating. Or rather, after we stopped, before we started again. But you remember."

He does. Another song comes on the radio. And she turns it up as if this comment meant nothing. Synthesizers and a guitar and a woman's soft, crooning voice fill the silence. An oldie, or a new song that sounds like an old song he can't place.

Vic rubs his jaw. "Yeah, I guess I do," he says. "But it seems worse suddenly."

Heather smiles. "He was better-looking back then, if you can recall. A total hunk like yourself. He'd just lost a pilot, some medical drama I don't think they ever even aired, to the director's cousin or something after a couple callbacks. You know the anxiety all that rejection can cause. His hair was puffy from being washed, practicing too much in the shower."

A laugh escapes from Vic. This did sound familiar.

The speedometer's needle continues its slow and arcing climb as the peaks of the mountain swell like the sharp wings of a great carrion bird about to flap and launch skyward.

"I'm serious," he says, trying to stifle himself.

"So am I," she says. "He was different then. Not to mention his big old dick."

"Heather!" Vic says.

"What?" she says. "You used to like when I talked like this."

"I did?"

"You *do*," she says.

"I do . . . Was he any good in bed?" he says.

"Oh, God, yes!" Heather glistens, sways, the dress shifting to reveal the whiter parts of her skin now. Circles of light grind across the ceiling as the wind continues to whip and tease her hair. "His dick would regenerate like a crab's claw," she continues.

"He could come and keep going and come again. Just keep growing back. In and out, in and out, all night. In, out, in, out, in, out, in, out. And for as long and as vigorous as you wanted. A freak of nature. I'm surprised you didn't hear us. Didn't he only live a few doors down from you?"

"I'm listening now," Vic says, pressing harder on the pedal. Pushing sixty in a curving forty zone. Sixty-five.

At this time of night, he knows, there won't be sirens. No cops. Not up over the ridge of the mountain, anyway. Or along the brief flatness before coming down. He isn't so paranoid anymore, while, in the distance, a starry landscape shines. A town. Their town. The life they'd chosen. Built for themselves. Their business that provides. But also glimmers like the sequins of Heather's dress.

"Keep talking," he says.

"I never came so hard," she says.

"Oh, yeah?" Vic speeds faster. Seventy now. But a seventy that feels like one hundred and ten. As he banks into turns, ghosting the median, the wheels about to give out as he moves through time. Gravel spraying. The twinkling light of the town shining in time with the familiar-unfamiliar music somehow, miraculously, while he hopes and prays to get home, with all of himself. Before whatever is happening wears off.

"More," he says. "Please. For the love of God. Don't stop."

The snow—a heavy blanket smothering roofs, roads, onion fields, pasture. But Vic's main concern is the roofs. He's brought along a twenty-three-year-old Junior to save his bad back a little pain by shoveling off those of his rentals before they collapse under all that weight. But first, a pit stop on the way.

The call came, unexpected, that morning. This opportunity from the sister, Inga, one-half inheritor of her family's Canadian timber fortune. Is Vic still available? Does he still have the plow? They'd almost forgotten about the house altogether. Turned out the bank didn't foreclose on their place after all. Left to sit for nearly a decade, she and her brother still own it: the Painted Lady. The one just up past Sooner's Orchard. Remember? Of course he does.

Junior rubs a porthole in the window and watches the orchards pass. The apple trees collect into gnarled, black cages on the hills. Even with chains on the truck's tires, the driving is slow, the road yet to be sufficiently plowed and salted.

"Are you even listening," Vic says to him. "I'm trying to teach you. Something important that'll supplement your interests. Keep your dreams afloat in desperate times. The customer doesn't buy your work. They buy you. You need to sell them. These people are rich. Crazy. The best kind."

"I thought they only called about a plow," says Junior, his breath pulsing across the frozen window.

Vic lowers his head to peer through the slot of visibility provided by the muttering dashboard defroster. "Never mind the plow. That's just getting your foot in the door," he says, and begins an outline of the work he's done for these people: the Olsen twins—Inga and Otto. Mythical people Junior has only heard rumors of.

"Carpentry, painting, yard work, gardening—you name it. Didn't matter," he continues. "Back then I was willing to do anything for a buck. Between your mother selling her vegetables and me painting houses, we could barely make our rehab loan payments. There was this urgency. They had me to work from the outside in. But disappeared before I could get to the inside part. Vanished. Still paid the down payment on my first rental property, though. Hell, they paid for your diapers. If you play your cards right, they'll pay for yours, too. Maybe another fixer-upper. Just wait. Soon enough you'll care plenty about *expenses*. These people really are crazy with money—when you can catch them . . ."

Through the porthole, Junior watches the apple trees drop away into seamless white horse pasture, the top rung of the fence riding above the snow alongside the road, bobbing and snaking with an unevenness accentuated by the flatness of the snow, his father talking still. Talking, talking, as always—trying to drag back to earth any daydream of a thought. Until an incomprehensible sound issues from Junior's mouth.

"Don't interrupt," Vic says.

"But the Sooner's barn—" says Junior.

"This is important—"

"Collapsed," continues Junior. "Completely gone. I hope Sooner managed to save the horses—"

"We're almost there and I'm trying to teach you something—"

But then Vic sees it, too. Or worse, yet, doesn't. Sooner's barn. Where it should be—where it isn't—has been replaced by a small mound of snow porcupined with jagged boards. Now he makes an incomprehensible sound himself, a clipped window of worry slamming shut.

"See," says Junior.

"I do," says Vic, already turning back to the wheel. "I'm sure Sooner put those horses up somewhere."

"Sooner doesn't even put up the dogs," says Junior.

"Never mind about the horses, never mind about the dogs," says Vic, and blinkers the turn signal. "We're here. Look alive." And with a mechanical whir, he engages the plow.

About half a mile off, the Painted Lady burns yellow against the snow. Vic works his way along the driveway whose bounds he must guess at with small bites from the plow. Swath after swath, he crushes the snow into berms, the distant farmhouse lurching higher with every bite into a sheer cliff of tri-colored peaks, a spectacle toward which they need to crane their necks. The detail truly something to admire. Its variety of shingle shapes—tears, spear-tips, hearts. Each painted a different color. Ornate molding, still somehow well-defined, as if milled yesterday. Even after all these years. The intricacy of trim, especially. Accentuated by Vic's brushwork. The way it snakes the yellow body with clashing colors of viridian and midnight blues, regal purples. Each shot through with one another. In conversation with the Victorian yellow. Each nook and turret, the balusters and façades.

"It's called a Painted Lady," Vic says, shifting the truck into *park*.

"You've told me that a thousand times," Junior replies.

Vic opens his mouth to say something about how the boy should be more grateful. That Vic didn't need to plow these people out, didn't need their money. Not only was he doing Junior a favor, he was sacrificing a good man. He couldn't justify paying Junior the kind of money these people could. Didn't Junior realize? Wasn't he mature enough now? He thought they'd grow past this indifference once he returned home from Costa Rica. If only he thought for just one second—

But then the porch's screen door shrieks open and a woman in a neon snowmobile suit steps, blinking, into the light. Through the icy porthole rubbed into Junior's window, Inga Olsen wades toward them, arms flailing for balance. A reflective patch on her arm glints in the morning light. She's waving something madly—a rubber-banded billfold—as if she might miss them.

Vic rolls down Junior's window to greet her with about as much haste. "Inga, it's been too long!" he says as she thrusts her red-chapped face into the cab of the truck.

Breathless, and with wide, lidless, blue eyes, she says, "Vic, you lifesaver! This snow . . . So unexpected. My brother and I. We were only passing through. We never intended to stay. We shared a sleeping bag on the floor."

"Not a problem," says Vic.

"*Not at all*," says Junior, chiming in like they'd talked about.

Inga removes her head from the truck, slips off a mitten. Pinching it between her neon yellow legs, she snaps off the rubber band from the billfold and begins unfurling money. After less than a second, however, she pauses. The idea of counting already seems to bore her. She holds out the entire wad.

Vic pushes her hand away. Laughs. "Don't insult me. Consider this a favor. I gave up plowing years ago. I only plow out my rentals now. Honestly, I just wanted the chance to show my son your place up close."

"How gracious of you," says Inga. "What a shame not to have finished!"

"Isn't it? Haunts me every day," says Vic.

"I've always imagined what it's like inside," says Junior.

"I always try to explain the grandeur," says Vic.

"I'm afraid we ran into family troubles up north, and never had the time," says Inga.

"A crying shame," says Vic, shaking his head.

"*A crying shame,*" says Junior, shaking his head too. A perfect mimic of his father when he wanted to be, a decent little actor.

Then Junior's digging a path toward the Painted Lady while Inga brings Vic up to speed.

Of course, she explains, inside it's only bones. Nothing new. Just like the day they had to let Vic go. Does Vic remember? Yes. Like it was yesterday. It was so hard to leave things unfinished like that. Six thousand square feet of nothing, atop fifteen acres. A daunting task. Over a century old. Would make a great bed-and-breakfast, though, if they could ever finish the inside.

But Vic's heard it all before. Seen it, too. And knows full well any renovations wouldn't be cost-effective. Nevertheless, entering the house, he *oohs* and *ahhs*. He makes these goals seem feasible. Unashamed of his melodrama, he chews the scenery, putting on a clinic for Junior in how to butter up a mark.

The screen door slaps shut behind them. And they stomp about the four-season porch, cleaning off their boots. While Junior leans his shovel against the wall, Vic shakes his head at the woodstove standing in the corner, large and black as the front of a freight train. "Someone should be warming their toes," he says.

Junior clicks his tongue in agreement as Inga calls into the house, "Otto, you'll never guess who stopped by for a visit," then beckons them to follow through a dark door. And sure enough, there's Otto, at a long oak table. Bald and thick-headed, in an identical snowmobile suit to his sister's. An egg held to one eye. Like some story his wife might've told a younger Junior at bedtime.

At first, he doesn't seem to notice them as they stand there without much else to look at—save the clouds of water-stain floating on the walls, the quiver of the dented copper ceiling in the camping stove's light, or the stove itself. On it, a pot of water boils. And in the pot, a rolling egg, a moist, pupilless eye.

Otto drops the another egg into the pot to warm before removing the first. He pinches the hot egg to his eye like a mono-cle. Then he looks up, unaffected by the heat, his exposed eye bulging in a kind of greeting.

"Otto!" Vic says. "Looking as fine as ever."

"God damn sties," Otto says to no one in particular.

"The Greeners popped in for a visit, dear," Inga says, as if he might not have noticed them yet.

"My son," says Vic.

"*Junior*," Junior says, holding out a hand that Otto ignores. "You have a wonderful home."

"Not *my* home," says Otto.

"I was trying to convince Vic we haven't forgotten this place, dear," says Inga. "That we'd turn it into a bed-and-breakfast sooner or later."

Otto adjusts the egg. "Pipe dreams," he says.

"I hope not," says Vic. "B&B's? A very lucrative business."

"*Very lucrative*," says Junior as Inga grabs his hand in her mitten.

"I promised I'd give this one a tour," she says, pulling Junior toward a wall of tall doors. Before which she stops a moment as if not knowing which to choose. She *eenie meenie miney moes*, then swings one open. Plunges inside. And as their footfalls fade away inside the Painted Lady, Vic takes the seat across from Otto, a silence taking hold.

And up from the silence, the moan of rusty door hinges. The burble of boiling water, a cauldron between them. The collision of their icy breaths.

Just being here—how easily the memories come back to Vic. How easily he can picture the arboretum in the summer, its domed glass ceiling withered with vines. The cavernous dining room and chandeliers, the sweeping stairwell and crown moldings. Almost as if he were with Inga now instead of Junior. Room after room, each interior windowless and dark. So dark at times Inga had to use a flashlight. The house still with no electric all those years ago.

"Six thousand square feet of nothing," he can almost hear her telling him, telling them. As she is surely telling his son for the second time, though he'd been little more than a newborn then. The dim shake of her flashlight on the wall, the creak of the floor. Empty and unfinished, every room. Full of possibilities. Its future branching out.

Not much later, they're back on their way, Vic and Junior—on route to the rentals. To deal with the snow. Same as before, but in a different sort of quiet. Behind a service truck now, laying out salt that crackles across the windshield. Otherwise not much else, save the mutter of the defroster.

Vic lowers his head to peer out. He steers the silence. And all this time, Junior's silent, too. Withholding. Vic waiting for the account. Waiting, and waiting—and finally, unable to take the waiting anymore, saying, "Well? How did it go?" Then for a moment, still, nothing. Just Junior's breath's heartbeat on the glass.

"If you're still worried about the horses . . ." Vic says.

"It's not the horses," Junior says. "And it's not the dogs."

"Then what?" says Vic.

"You'll never believe me—"

"Just tell me. I'm your father—"

"I saw something," Junior says. "An old woman. Inside the house."

"An old woman?" Vic says with a laugh. "Probably just their mother. Inga said she was sick. Didn't she—"

"I knew you wouldn't listen—"

"I am listening," Vic says. "Go ahead. Have at it."

And Junior does. He turns to him, eyes wide and animal-scared. "Fine, all right. Inga was giving me the tour. I was really working her. Really, I was. *Oohs* and *ahhs*, just like you said. You'd be proud. She must have gotten turned around. 'I haven't been here in years,' she said. Something wasn't right. But we continued. We continued, and cobwebs brushed my scalp. The ground dipped soft beneath our feet. Rot crept into my nose. The house, a maze. We were lost—"

"Jesus Christ—"

"But Inga must've thrown open the wrong door. Obviously, she'd made a mistake, the way she reacted. She didn't want me to see. Slammed the door shut. But over her shoulder, I saw an old woman. Like I said. But maybe not how you imagine. Older. Dressed in a thin nightgown. A ghost, at first. Goose pimples broke out. Then I heard the beeping of machines. I felt the tropical warmth of the heaters from within the room. The radio played scratchy classical music. A bedpan and a wheelchair. A hospital bed. Insulated windows. I know what I saw. I saw her face. A mosaic of wrinkles and fear. Dead, but still alive, this woman—"

"What are you even saying—" says Vic.

"Aren't you listening?" says Junior.

"And all this in one glance?"

"Yes, all at once. But what's more? The worst part—"

"Let's hear it—"

"A chain. A chain running from her wheelchair to the steam heater. I saw it. They were keeping her there. Those freaks—"

"The way you talk. God. You remind me of your mother—"

"You said you'd listen—"

"I never said I'd believe you—"

"They're keeping her hostage. I'm sure of it. That old woman is a captive. We need to call Social Services. The police. Someone!"

"First Sooner's horses, now this? Give me one good reason. Some real evidence. God, this is some story you're writing. Maybe your finest."

"Money. Inbreeding. Who knows?" says Junior.

"But they don't even have electric, son. I worked there for years. Years and I never saw an old lady. It's just a spooky old house. Your imagination's just run wild—"

"Go back and check the electric box if you don't believe me!" says Junior. "Go back and check!" But Vic's heard enough. He isn't going to waste his valuable time on these theatrics. These *conspiracies* of an immature mind. Not another second of his life. What value could be gleaned from this? It's so early, and there are roofs piled with snow. Obviously, there must be some reasonable explanation, some misunderstanding.

Junior will talk himself out soon enough, he thinks. And sure enough, Junior does. After a while, the truck falls back into a silence. Just the crackling of salt. The dashboard defroster. The freeze creeping fingers across the glass. Junior's silence growing louder by the mile. Save for his scribbling on his notepad.

In the paper the next week, there's a news report: Sooner's horses killed. Three Clydesdales. A mule. "I told you," Junior says, driving the truck on the way to another job. But this proves nothing to Vic. Nothing about an old woman, anyway. No scandal in their small town. No car that visits the Painted Lady at night, bringing food and meds for the alleged captive. No reason to suspect, aside from what Junior couldn't have seen. No proof. Vic never stops to check if the electric meter is turned on. Refuses. There isn't even an investigation into the Sooner's neglect of the horses. The humane society doesn't even take the dogs.

After a while, Junior stops bringing it up altogether. And after another year or so of this, he moves off somewhere against Vic's better judgment. Amid a global financial crisis, no less. High unemployment, low wages, and little opportunity—the opposite of what Vic offered. The literal worst time to chase your dreams. Which, for Junior, meant little more than working on a paint crew in order to buy enough time to scratch off his stories. Upstate. Out of state. Having learned nothing from Vic. A lost cause. Gone.

The years trail away in a white flurry. The Painted Lady languishes deeper into decay from the inside out. The Olsens never do call about the work. Even from the road, it's obvious. On the way to the rentals. Junior off and married now, a child of his own coming any day, no doubt, to shake him awake, help him understand the sacrifices Vic's made. Now it's just Vic who passes, on his way to fix a faucet at another rental, to patch a cracked wall.

To keep up with appearances and collect the rent. Shovel snow. But in silence now. Heather continues to urge him to hire out. To assemble a reliable crew. But he doesn't want to waste the money. He has no one to talk to and the Painted Lady is slipping fast. Like him. Once so glorious on the outside, but now sinking more and more into oblivion. The balusters rotting. Four-season porch bowing deep. The paint shivering off into the weedy gardens. His master paint job from long ago all for nothing. The colors falling out of conversation now, almost unrecognizable. The house festering in ways only the rich and crazy can allow. Such grand decay, against all he stands for. A part of Vic wants to fix the place up for free, put things back in order, where they belong. If only his back were better, he thinks. If only he were not so tired all the time.

Each time he passes, it's the same. The daydream. In it, he stops, shoulders open the door to save the old woman inside from her captivity. Junior was right, it turns out, all those years ago. His son, more attentive than him, more observant than even his wife. Vic bolt-cuts the chain, then carries the old woman out the door draped in his arms. A hero. An apology. She's nearly one hundred now, but still alive. Summer, spring, fall, regardless. In the daydream, it's always snowing. Always there's a news report, an article in the paper. Vic's a hero. A handsome hero. His wife wraps him in her arms. The Olsens had been keeping their mother there, it explains, to drain her money. A dispute over the inheritance. All that wealth a corruption. The incestuous couple rotting in prison now because of him. The town will hold a parade in Vic's honor. And when the day comes Junior's there. They clap each other on the back, reunited on a float that rides past Sooner's freshly raised barn. After all these years: Father, son, among the waving people. The bugle of a brass band. Heather there in her glittering vintage dress while the raining confetti mixes with the snow around them, leeching into it, dying it colors. So much confetti that somebody, somewhere, at some point, will have to plow.

WHICH ONE WERE YOU?

The drive there always freaks him out. Something about the way the country highway's pattern of overgrown campgrounds, boarded-up motels, and stretches of impenetrably dark woods reminds him of childhood. The way the area seems quagmired in foreclosures that, he knew, no amount of labor could fix up. Or the way the halogen-lighted church always rips out of the darkness like an oversize knife. After a while, it all resembles a series of childhood memories fused with horror movie sets.

Whatever it is, Junior doesn't like it. Almost as much as he doesn't like not being productive. If he's not painting a house or working on his novel, an idle itchiness overtakes his body. That's all to say since the start of his wife's, Caity's, pregnancy, whenever his childhood friend Vince asked to meet up, Junior had an excuse handy: working that weekend, writing events, a doctor's visit, or nonexistent dinner plans. Only this time, Caity'd overheard the call in progress and intervened, insisting he should go.

"Don't be ridiculous. I'm not due for another eight weeks," she said, loud enough for Vince to hear. "For Christ's sake, go and have some fun."

Now Junior pulls into the parking lot the church shares with an enormous prefab building of black corrugated steel: *SKATE TIME.* Off and on, every few years, for what seems like decades, he's been coming here to meet him, to this building in the middle of nowhere with a skating rink and a skate park inside.

Junior drives a few laps around the parking lot, searching for his thirty-three-year-old friend's still-after-all-these-years skate-stickered car. But all the cars are stickered here: *Fear God and*

Repent. John 3:16. How long can you ignore the Holy Ghost? And it's hard to differentiate these from a Thrasher logo in the dark.

He parks, sits with the motor running, and calls Vince to see where he is. But the service keeps dropping out. The radio stations continually looping back to the same one: gospel, a baritone heralding the birth of a son over sad slide guitar. Five more minutes, and five more. Then, reluctantly, Junior steps out into the parking lot.

Since he can remember, it's always been the same guy behind the counter—this middle-aged man with a soul patch, a solemn demeanor Junior always associated with the suicidal tendencies of the Pacific Northwest—working around the clock. Yet, tonight, there is a different man: younger, though similar in demeanor, with ripped-off sleeves and precise burns on each joint of his hands, like he recently pressed them (or had them pressed) flat to a hot skillet.

"What have they got you doing back there!?" Junior tries to joke with him.

"Dry skin," the young man says without laughing. "How can I help?"

It's hard to imagine where all these people come from. Having only just driven such a stretch of desolate highway, they all somehow feel more like ghosts, Junior thinks, watching the hundred plus teenagers orbit the rink's glossy surface. Full of a youth the men hanging their wrists over the barricade seem to have gathered to stare at. Bug-lighted by these young girls (their daughters?) and their towering John Deere boyfriends with their tanned arms hooked around bare shoulders, the flushed cheeks, the beginning lust of romance.

Junior notices an old man in a trench coat who spins alone at the center of their orbit. Like this pivot point of the entire slow-moving mass. A white, Godly beard fogging a smile that seems to mark all of them. A smile that Junior's come to associate with family, and now with a cult. As if suddenly these people were all on the brink of some awful ceremony, and at any minute, the old man's ragged hands would raise to exalt a beating human heart toward the fiberglass skylight and its waning autumn moon.

Now Junior sits at a circular table by the arcade with his skateboard across his lap. He checks his cell phone again: no service, no calls. For, while the roller rink is packed, the skate park is empty, like it's always been, save this one little boy with a helmet on and no skateboard he can discern. He's too embarrassed to skate by himself. With this little boy. *I should've stayed home*, he thinks, *and tried to write*.

The boy's mother watches her son from behind a plexiglass wall as he gallops up and down the ramps, braying like a horse. Her face—the love described there in its softness scares Junior to observe: aching and sweet. If he ever feels that, he's sure, his heart will burst right out of his chest for the old man to hold up to the moon.

He texts Vince again: *Did you hear? Skate Time keeps horses now?*

Did you hear? The skate park has been replaced by a bible camp?

Did you?

Did you?

Vince?

But the texts keep coming back.

Maybe it's the cistern of sweating milk on the concession stand's counter, or his frustration at having to skateboard alongside a child, or the apparent growing popularity of roller skates, or the look on the mother's face, but each time a siren goes off in the arcade, Junior can't help but reach for his cell phone.

He checks the time to discover Vince isn't as late as he feels: only ten minutes now.

Between songs, the deejay speaks deeply into the microphone. He plays Whitney Houston, Diana Ross, the Beach Boys, the Eagles (a band his father often played while they worked). Each time Junior looks toward the concession stand, the new guy behind the counter with the burnt knuckles knows every word. He smiles, looks at his phone again: a picture of his wife and two Chihuahuas, all three fragile heads titled at him in curiosity. Still serviceless. No texts, no calls.

After a while, Junior gets up, goes to the bathroom despite not having to go.

Here, he runs into the trench-coated old man at the urinal, peeing without any hands. He cups the back of his bald head, elbows out, sighing. The stream sounds heavy. And Junior finds that he can't pee until the old man is gone.

When he gets back, Vince is there, waiting. Like he's been there all along. "Where have you been," he says. "Cutting it up on the roller rink?" Then he laughs in this way that causes Junior to laugh too. To suddenly feel not so scared and old. Like the old man in the trench coat had made a signal and a glass tube slid down from out of the sky and sucked Junior up, transporting him back to his youth.

Now they enter the skate park area, an oversize setup of raw plywood meant more for rollerblades and bikes. They ride up and down the ramps on what Junior has come to refer to as "his useless wooden toy," trying to remember the tricks they used to do. They fall and laugh at the minor pain within their bodies.

After a while, the little helmeted boy retreats to the corner as they read the rules written there on the wall for the thousandth time:

DO NOT SPIT. They spit.

DO NOT CURSE. They curse.

DO NOT DISRESPECT. They dance mockingly to "Boogie Shoes."

Until, suddenly, it's so funny now, hilarious. *Why don't I do this more often?* Junior thinks. And all this time, the little helmeted boy watches them from his corner. No longer does he gallop up and down the ramps. No longer does he bray. He just stands there in the corner, with candy-stained lips, while, from behind the plexiglass, his mother watches with her fixed, dreamy gaze and cult-smile. While the old man in the trench coat continues to spin the roller rink's entire mass with his gravity.

"I wonder if the original cashier killed himself," Junior says. Then, "You should have heard that little kid braying before—I don't know how long I'd be able to put up with that."

He skateboards and slashes the coping with his truck. He rips around the park's ramps, skimming the concrete with his hand like he's surfing. A little looser now. Sometimes even landing the tricks he'd intended. "Remember that one time?" he says and remembers what he's always forgetting: why he drives out here. Through those nightmare towns of foreclosures and memories of thankless work. The fun he has.

Afterward, they sit in the seating area by the arcade—laughing about old times, remembering when—when the little boy comes up to them. He still has the helmet on. Junior still can't tell if something is wrong with him or not. "Hello?' he says. "Hi there."

The little boy toes an invisible rock.

"Hi . . ."

Finally, the little boy speaks, barely audible, a red grime of candy coating his lips and tongue: "Which one were you in there?"

"Excuse me?"

"Which one were you?"

"Which one was I?" Junior says, laughing. "I was me—" he says, but senses the insufficiency of his answer and stops short. Now it's his turn to toe the invisible rock: a husband, a soon-to-be father, a son? A would-be writer? A painting contractor? More his mother or father? An infinitely small link in an infinite chain . . . heading toward what? No, given the circumstances, his answer was too much and not nearly enough.

"Which one were you?" the little boy says again, in a way that seems to confirm that, yes, Junior's answer had been insufficient. That he required another, truer response. His mother stands behind him, smiling that same cult-smile with lipstick on her teeth. Expectant as her son. Like his answer could ruin them all.

"What'd he say?" Vince says with a laugh, seeming to notice the little boy for the first time. A siren jolts the moment, one of the arcade machines paying out a John Deere boyfriend with tanned arms. Blue-and-red lights rub the carpeted walls of the roller rink behind them as the little helmeted boy continues staring, toeing that invisible rock. Junior senses the roller-skating orbit slowing to stare at him, too. Waiting for his answer.

Did they turn the music down? Dim the lights? A chill creeps along his neckline.

A new song starts: "Mambo No. 5." The new cashier is no longer mouthing the words, and the little helmeted boy persists:

"Which one were you, which one were you, which one were you?" he says.

Panicking now, Junior looks toward the arcade's flashing lights, thinking how to answer. The sirens continue. The deejay speaks more deeply now, the words foreign-sounding. As more man wrists hang over the barrier. More arms hook over the shoulders of their daughters. Vince laughs harder now—louder, as he prays for the little helmeted boy to gallop away with his smiling mother.

But the little boy just keeps standing there, toeing that invisible rock, awaiting Junior's answer. A reflective strip on his Velcro sneakers catching the arcade's strobing light. At which, Junior shakes his head, blinks his eyes, unable to clear his vision.

I swear to God, he thinks, *the little helmeted boy is lifting off the ground, levitating right there, right now, before me. A full inch. An inch and a half. Two inches now. A miracle*, he thinks. *An answer, a sign.* "Which one were you?" And Junior shakes his head some more. He blinks his eyes, desperate to clear them.

Married forty years today, Heather and Vic play that game. After dinner, in their California king with the lights off and no TV on because: special occasion. Where they take turns confessing things one might not know about another: how Heather once French kissed her second cousin. Or that Vic fooled around with his roommate in college. The threesome Heather had with those football players, linebackers from a visiting team she can't remember. The time Vic saw his childhood neighbor making love to a cow. Had Vic told her about the cow already? Well, she'd told him about the football players, too.

"What else?" The game goes into a dying fall with the realization they've traded these true stories before. And what's worse? That they had forgotten certain trades. The forgetting and the remembering: now just one more pattern they've fallen into. Like the annual trip to the Italian restaurant, Vic's gift of antique jewelry, or Heather's vintage dress. The extra glass of wine to prime themselves for the lovemaking to follow, tedious now at the advent of retirement. Without another foreclosure on the horizon, and Heather sinking ever deeper into her garden—everything feels like another beat of the same.

Not to mention, boy, does Vic need to urinate. His bladder: full of celebratory wine. But he refuses to get up and relieve himself out of fear that Heather will turn on the TV and return them to their usual routine. Which, paradoxically, he finds, is all he really wants. But he hates himself for this: wanting to urinate and watch TV instead of making love to his wife of four decades.

So, to save the moment, Vic decides to tell her: a story, he explains, that he's buried so deep, for so long, that its exhumation feels less like something he decides to do and more something he realizes he has in him. "This one I know you haven't heard," he says.

Did she remember when he painted that old general's lake house up in the Adirondacks? Before he'd started working for those incestuous twins? When they were saving up for the house after they decided to stay in the Victorian? That friend of a friend of her mother's? When he had to camp out in the yard and bathe in the lake because the general wouldn't let him inside?

"Of course—" she says.

That humid summer they sunk their money into fixing up that rotten bungalow? And Junior wasn't talking, still, and they thought he'd contracted Lyme meningitis?

"I said I remember."

"I'm sorry," he says. He just wanted to put the story into the proper context. Otherwise, she might misinterpret what he'd done. Might not forgive him.

Okay—what had he done?

Most of that day, Vic spent touching up. He knocked on the general's front door around noon, expecting to be paid. But instead of the check—which the general made a point of writing out in front of him—he was handed a punch list full of bitchery and tedium: slightly jagged lines he'd cut, hairline cracks he'd left uncaulked. Lead paint chips scattered about in the gardens.

So, a couple of hours later, after ticking off each item, he knocked again. Once, twice, three times. No answer. Which was weird, because every time he'd knocked before, the general had opened the door immediately, as if he'd been standing guard behind it.

Cheap bastard, Vic thought, and tried the handle. The door creaked open—much to his surprise—onto the foyer from which the dark hallway branched. He stepped into the hall after making his presence known, calling, "Anybody home." Then he walked down the hallway until it gave way to a high-ceilinged living room flooded with crimson dusk. He still remembers the way the woods burned through every window, the way the general sat there in a bathrobe, his white hair appearing to burn, too, as he watched TV with these enormous headphones on.

"All finished," Vic said, stepping into the general's line of sight. He waved a hand, waiting to be noticed. Then again, faster. "All finished!" he said, still waving. Yet, no matter what he did, he couldn't seem to capture the old man's attention. He just continued to stare right through him, a softness to his eyes, a vagueness. Until, suddenly, those eyes sharpened into an accusatory glare, as if he'd just caught Vic midburglary and was about to leap to his feet to dispatch a series of ass-kicks.

So imagine Vic's surprise when, instead of berating him, the general removed the headphones and offered him a pleasant, dentured smile. "From such a dour man, I swear to God, it felt obscene!" he says. The way the blue TV light played on his teeth as the dusk burned like neon in his white hair. The headphones whining in his lap. The mosquitoes the sound conjured, the itchy bites that plagued him throughout that dreadful week.

"Cynthia?" the general said and squinted up at him. "Honeybee?"

"It's Vic Greener," Vic said, embarrassed for this old man. Who'd probably strung up Mussolini during WWII. This decorated man of honor, rising sweetly out of a dream about his dead wife, an old lover, a dear friend—back into the cold, harsh, lonely words of his life—because if there was a wife or lover or friend, Vic hadn't seen them. No one had come or gone from the house all week. "All finished," he said.

Nevertheless, the general persisted: "Cynthia? Cynthia? Cynthia? Honeybee?" he said. Until, unable to take any more of this, Vic walked over and turned on the light to rouse the General back to his senses.

"Cynthia!?" the general said again, but different now, not so sleepy looking anymore in the light—but alarmingly awake. While his face remained peaceful, the rest of his body appeared taut, straining. Sweat pearled on his cheeks and forehead. The cords raised in his neck as if attempting to lift the slack peacefulness of his still-smiling face back into its usual scowl. "Pudding Cup!?"

Soon, it became obvious to Vic that something had happened to the old man—correction: was *happening* to the old man. Inside him. Something dire. And Vic rushed off in search of a landline, finding a rotary phone fixed to the wall. He turned the dial to nine. To one—

And it's here Vic wants Heather to remember their financial hardships at the time. Their fledgling real estate business, the ongoing renovations. And Junior, their fragile little boy. How he'd been bitten by that tick and couldn't put his chin to his chest, with an infection ratcheting itself up his spine. The real possibility of losing everything. He wants her to remember all of this, when he tells her that, instead of turning the rotary dial one last time, he placed the phone back on the wall.

Could Heather remember how it was? Did she understand the whys? The backstory? Did she believe him? And if not, after all these years, did she really think his imagination was rich enough to make this up? She doesn't say one way or another. Her expression, like her silence, remains impossible to read in the dark.

Well, anyway, Vic continues, the general's eyes had closed. But behind their wrinkled shells, they continued to roll. So Vic shook him. "Wake up," he said, and shook him again, hard. "I'm going to help you. But I need you to pay me."

Now, the general's breath rasped in and out. "Please," Vic said, still shaking him. A dying man. Shaking him and pleading with his slack body. Until, suddenly, a floorboard creaked, tearing his gaze away toward the sound. Where he half-expected to discover the old general's wife, Cynthia. To find his Pudding Cup standing there in her robe in the dying light, trembling, afraid for her life, accusing him of killing the man, attempting to burglarize their home. "Cynthia?" he called into the house. No response. Again and again: nothing. And when he looked back, the general had stilled, found peace. His eyes: no longer moving. The headphones whined in his dead lap.

After gathering himself, the first thing Vic remembers doing was shutting off all the lights. Powering off the TV whose light danced on the general's face, resurrecting it, on the off chance that they few neighbors might catch him as he stalked about the house, as dusk turned to night.

The drawers first, then the cabinets. Then the drawers again. The kitchen closet, the coffee table. Shaking out the few magazines neatly stacked there—he cased every nook and cranny the kitchen had to offer, discovering nothing but bills and loose hard candies. And with those options exhausted, what else was left but to search the general himself?

He had no other choice, remember? Their predicament back then? His toothpaste commercial money spent? The check, he'd thought, must be inside his bathrobe pocket. He leaned in, sniffing the air. The general smelled funny—he'd soiled himself, Vic realized. He still remembers the way the odor wafted up, sweet and fetid while Vic patted him down. The empty pockets. The invisible mosquitoes that buzzed around his own neck and removing his hand to slap them, then cursing softly and looking around the living room.

"Cynthia?" Vic remembers saying aloud again. No, of course Vic didn't want to go upstairs. Didn't even intend to, really. Until, then, without really thinking, he was tiptoeing up the stairs, looking for that check. Or, okay, he'll admit it, maybe looking for something else now, of equal value. Something to bring home for his family. Jewelry, perhaps. Antiques. Bond certificates. He didn't know what. Just that he—*they*—needed the money.

Remember? As he continued upward, he certainly did, moving carefully up the steps so as not to release any of the noise they held. Down the bare hallways and toward the bedrooms to see what he could find. "Okay, fine, steal," he says. "Steal from a dead man—"

Did Heather even want to know what he'd found? Did she want to know why he'd kept this from her for so long? He looks at her, trying to read her expression across the width of their California king. A smile? He doesn't know. It's still too dark. His wife: too quiet. Does she believe him? Does she not find the circumstances as damning as he thought?

In this way, her movement toward him makes no sense, either. As, accompanied by a slight jingle from the bracelet he'd given her as an anniversary present, she reaches for him. Touches his face. Finds his mouth. The same as always, yet alien with passion. Her body moving differently, too, through the dark. Through the years. Her vintage dress sliping off, thrown off the bed to the floor. Her body on his. Hot. Different with fervor. Younger. Someone else maybe. "Heather?" he says.

"Honeybee," she says, nibbling an ear lobe. "Pudding cup," she says, shoving her index finger into his mouth.

Afterward, Vic rolls off her, somewhat embarrassed but also satisfied. Happy to have revived something by separating themselves enough to come together again. To reignite that initial spark with his morbid confession. He stumbles off toward the bathroom, over their cast-off clothes and shoes, his heart aching with excitement in his chest.

How long might the feeling last? he wonders as his fingers dust the wall for a light switch, a doorknob. He shuffles along in this state of confusion, trying to preserve this part of him, which so rarely reaps up and offers so little to hang on to—

Then *bang*! He stubs his toe on the TV stand, and curses: a soft *motherfucker*, on account of the pain, but also at the realization: Now, what other stories are left for him to give?

In the dark, he trips again. Cursing louder now as he continues toward the darker rectangle of the bathroom's entrance, its black mouth waiting, yawning. And Vic: too afraid to ask Heather to turn on the TV or bedside lamp, of the condition she might find him in once the room went bright.

HOUSE CEREMONY

A Catskill varmint hotel turned quaint summer cabin. A half-charred farmhouse hiked up on carjacks overhauled into a popular farm-to-table restaurant. A haunted gingerbread with a basement full of graves, exorcised and revitalized as a church. A successful career by any measure. Four decades of hard work Vic Greener's family can look back on with pride.

Nevertheless, not six months into retirement, under the auspices of picking up a new Weedwacker string, Vic visits another auction, bids on a recent foreclosure in a lusting fit. His heart romance-thudding over the wretched remains of a hunting lodge in Pond Eddy—a crooked one-story with the moldiest cedar shake siding. And this despite his promise to Heather that he's done with work. Free to take walks and help harvest freakish vegetables from her garden. To take trips on the occasional Sunday to visit their son—or anywhere for that matter. "I'll go to Europe! I'll go to Africa! Asia isn't off the table!" he's claimed more than once. Whatever she wanted. She could seal him in vinegar and place him in the cupboard to float among the other vegetables she's canning, if that's her prerogative.

But then the silences between the auctioneer's calls for the opening bid work Vic's hand up like a ratchet—past his shoulder, his ear, where his flowing hair once was.

Heather will understand, he thinks as he pays the deposit. He'd have been a fool, crazy even, if he didn't steal this potential gold mine.

From the auction house, Vic sets off straight for his new ward. He considers picking Heather up. Not too long ago, she would've wanted to come along, would've been there every step of the way. But lately she'd started calling his work ethic suicidal: "You're seventy-five years old with a pancake heart!"

"Who're you doing this for?" she'd continue. "Where's *more* going to take you but to an early grave? Look around—we've succeeded at a decent shot at enjoying the twilight of our life. Even the dying part, thanks to advances in modern medicine. You can afford to suffer your last breath in the comfort of your own home, if you choose to. Still with some legacy leftover to pass down to your son. And your son's soon-to-be-born daughter: her first car, a decent college fund. No question. This isn't for us, or for Junior, not anymore, I know that much. Don't worry about him. He'll figure it out."

Well, maybe she didn't speak that last part directly. Instead, she conveyed it through the image of himself reflected in her dark eyes. An experience that, since day one, instilled the same panic. The same anxiety he'd suffered so many sweaty nights as a struggling actor—the actor's dream, where he's forgotten his lines and the other actor onstage refuses to help him. And the play just keeps going. On and on.

So, Vic follows the GPS alone. Past the charming village that's developed over the years. With its overpriced restaurants and tchotchke shops. To where the town transitions into sprawling, vinyl-sided developments. And then farther into field and pasture. Miles of bramble and woodland. Pond Eddy.

The GPS cuts out, and Vic reduces his speed. Squints out the passenger-side window into a wall of gray brush, hoping to approximate the driveway's location. Until, finally, he does—or thinks he does, anyway. He turns down a constricted gullet of overgrowth, the light dimming as if the sunglasses he'd perched atop his head had fallen across his eyes. They hadn't.

Branches rake the doors. The truck rocking over potholes. The radio cutting in and out. The air in the cab: bog-like and salted. Vic wonders if he's taken a wrong turn. Maybe he's gone down a fire road or a hunting trail—

But then, behold: the distant hunting lodge, caked in grime and jagged like a roan tooth. Irresistible with its moldy cedar shakes and mossy, sloughing roof. Its mustache of dead hedges bristling along the stone foundation.

Vic pulls closer, parks. Sits for a minute, waiting for shutters to straighten, the roof to unslough. For mold to vanish and sunlight to pour through trimmed trees and dry that swamped-up yard. To color in these drained flower beds. But no visions come. Excitement congeals into a sludge of what had been the bubbling caldron of his chest.

"Talk to me," he says and steps out into frothy mud and dead silence, as if his mere presence would call the house to attention, correct its slumping posture.

Historically, Vic has been inclined to depict these undertakings as mountains he and Heather can only scale together. Something to connect over. But that night at dinner he downplays the summit ahead. "Not even much to clear out," he tells her. "A few boxes, a torn armchair. A stained carpet in need of pulling up. Bones in good shape, though."

Vic pauses so Heather can comment on potential paint palettes and landscaping designs, new ways to modernize something so campy and old, like she always does. So Heather can construct the setting in which their success will play out. Heather, however, remains as silent as that hunting lodge. She pokes at her plate of boiled chicken and the green beans she makes for his heart health.

"We could flip this thing in our sleep—" Vic says.

Now his throat hitches at the dread her furrowed face then mirrors back to him, as if she'd been there with him, imagined what he'd felt: the kaleidoscopic slurry of spiderwebs that dragged across his scalp. The demonic breeze that fluted through the rooms after he opened the windows. The dizzying stench that never evacuated, radiating from that oblong stain on the carpet like a pulse. All of it seems to tally into her fearful expression.

Vic regards his boiled chicken. The green beans, the wild rice. Raises his utensils. Eats. He thinks of those tuning forks they'd bought for Junior (before he gave up whatever instrument he supposedly needed them for to pursue a "writing career") rusting somewhere in the basement now. They wouldn't resonate the way they used to. And somewhere along the way, he and Heather had fallen out of sync too.

Vic wakes early. He's dressed and out the door before Heather can force the scrambled egg whites with cubed sweet potatoes she's cooking on him. He drives through town, singing with the radio. Glad for the approaching workday and feeling none of last night's dread. None of the boredom of the last six months. No longer old and ready to be forgotten in the cupboard, Vic is still healthy, still muscled, considering. With more than a few years of triumphs in the name of his family's future left.

He sings past the tchotchke shops, past the developments: a country song about a sexy tractor, another about a silver stallion. Into the expanse of land and farms, where the onion fields stretch in stagnant black lakes to the valley's rim. Elvis and Jesus, the Mexican migrants he'd hired as helpers soon after Junior's departure, live here in a trailer on the farthest edge of the valley. Just past the farmhouse Vic still owns. He'd called them yesterday, even before calling Heather. They're cousins, with wide, brown faces scuzzed with thin beards and topped with shaggy black hair he'd only ever seen crushed beneath baseball caps. They've worked with Vic for years now and know his appreciation for promptness. They're already outside waiting when he pulls up.

They say their hellos and pile into the truck three across—Elvis, in the middle, squats over the center console with his shoulders politely tucked. "I thought you retired," he says. "I thought you said no more work."

Vic laughs. "You must be confusing me with my wife."

Then everything falls silent, save the song on the radio: "Before He Cheats."

Followed by "I Hope You Dance."

Then "Save a Horse (Ride a Cowboy)."

And finally "Tequila Makes Her Clothes Fall Off."

Until this, too, cuts out into static.

The spiderwebs are fewer today. The wind less demonic. But the carpet smell has worsened. The smell has its own texture of urgency. Of bacterial warfare. Or as if it's dredging the concern Heather reflected at Vic last night by inducing a headache no amount of Advil can now dislodge. Her look said, "Poor Vic, I've seen how this plays out."

Instead of poking through boxes for anything of value, Vic joins the relay to the truck, waddling out the furniture that cluttered the lodge, anything he can carry to get the reeking carpet up that much faster, in hopes of ridding the hunting lodge of that God-awful stench. Back and forth, back and forth, heaving breath—sweat drips down Vic's creased face, stings his eyes. His exertion mixed with the carpet's smell tightens his brain like a knot.

They might've had the carpet up by noon if the bottom of the boxes didn't keep giving out. The soggy flaps of cardboard keep opening like trapdoors, spilling distractions across the floor: strangely shaped pillows, what appears to be a studded dog collar. A short paddle embossed with the word *smile*. These greasy magazines whose covers Elvis and Jesus couldn't help but laugh at:

A nude bottle-blonde splay-legged on the hood of a muscle car.

A leather-clad woman spitting fire.

A gimp with a zippered mouth.

It's not the weirdest set of forgotten stuff they've seen over the years. Just another window into someone else's life, as far as Vic's concerned. But Heather would've combed through them not very long ago with excitement in her eyes.

The day's heat has only amplified the carpet's smell. And Vic drops into the closest seat to catch his breath: this mealy armchair in the center of the room. He crunches its springs, tilts his head back, and pinches his nose. He almost calls out to Heather to bring him some lemonade, then catches himself. Instead, he just repeats to Elvis and Jesus, "Keep working, I'm all right. Go on now."

All day, it's like this: Vic's head throbbing, his heart working overtime, the heat pouring like gasoline on the ten-alarm fire of the carpet's smell. Elvis and Jesus in and out, the rotten boxes spilling more magazines and sex toys. More dildos. More ropes. Unlabeled VHS tapes packaged and stamped for mailing. Lots of them. Too many to count. Stacks of papers. Names and addresses. Spreadsheets covered in matrices of numbers that Vic takes to be financial records. A length of barbed wire. And much more like this, each item causing uneasy laughter to travel through them—

Around three o'clock, when they've reached the farthest of the boxes and one releases a flood of envelopes full of Polaroids on the wretched carpet, the mood darkens. Their laughter stops. Elvis pours out an envelope's worth and fans out the Polaroids while Jesus flips over the ones that land face down. They hand Vic another stuffed envelope. The first few Polaroids he pulls out are not unlike some of himself and Heather from their first anniversary, one of the few vacations they'd taken over the years: a trip to the desert. The photos buried, somewhere in their closet. But then Vic stops flipping: No, these weren't like their hidden Polaroids at all.

Vic leans back into the armchair, considers the ramification of reporting the Polaroids. What he suspects was going on back here, the evil business. The police tape and procedure, the police cars that'd rut up the wet yard. All the chaos, the damage. The delay in his profits over what may not even be anything at all.

It's true—the age of young people has grown difficult for him to decipher in recent years. Everyone looks younger to him now. And anyway, don't the young people willfully do these things nowadays? Regardless, the evidentiary chain is sure to clasp his renovation to a halt. "Just throw these out," he says finally, tossing the stack back into the pile. "All of them."

Elvis and Jesus do so hastily, without question, as if unable to rid themselves of these photographs fast enough, doing their best not to look at the images as they work. But after the last of the

Polaroids have been tied away into garbage bags, the dark mood they'd brought into the room remains—the previous owner's enterprise still haunts the place.

They handle the few remaining boxes with too much care, too slowly, unwilling to risk any more exposure. Vic remains in the chair. He rubs his scalp, glares into his serviceless phone, wanting and not wanting to call Heather. To quench his thirst with her ice-cold lemonade. He wonders if he should, in fact, inform the police of the apparent crimes they'd discovered. Or even, at a bare minimum, check if the monster who'd owned this place is still alive. No, he shouldn't. The perpetrator is surely dead, he thinks—just look around. The must, the mold, the water damage—the house has clearly sat vacant for decades. And who could say it was even the owner who took them, anyway?

He cycles through these thoughts until the thick canopy of trees brings down a premature night and no calls have been made. The workday is done, the next day fast approaching. And he'll have to exorcise the carpet tomorrow.

"I've got a hunch we'll discover hardwood. Something we can buff out, brighten the place up."

Leftovers tonight. Yesterday's boiled chicken and green beans. The same uneaten plate before Heather, the same concern wrinkling her brow. But she's more exhausted this time. As if she too had spent the day dizzied by the rancid stench of the carpet, the sight of the depraved Polaroids that made his stomach go cold. She can't seem to lift the fork to her mouth.

Vic longs for the time Heather would've had a catalog ready, tagged with photos of pinecone cabinet knobs for them to consider, her face lit up over an antler chandelier to complement the hardwood floor. For the rest of the night, they would've talked and talked, honing their attack plan, building, there in the imaginary space between them, the renovated house their buyer was somewhere dreaming of.

However, tonight Heather isn't silent so much as she is anti-verbal—so unlike his wife of forty years. She stares and chews and sips her water without expressing any curiosity about his first day with the hunting lodge. Doesn't even try to reason with him. But Vic knows enthusiasm for their old life, their livelihood, can't be killed so easily after only a few short months of retirement. And he misses this aspect, their partnership, their collaboration, so much he almost tells her about the stench, the stain on the floor, the trapdoors in the boxes. The sex toys—maybe the Polaroids. Anything to shake her from this troubling quiet. After the flip, there'd be plenty of time to do whatever she wanted!

But he can't push the words through his lips, stymied by the strands of anxiety Heather twists into her hair. It's as if she'd witnessed the same defilement and filth he had that day. Or worse—as if she's already seen what lies ahead.

Vic doesn't remember his bed, this California king. The exhaustion of the previous day remains with him, like a sickness, pinning him there beside his wife. He can't seem to cut through the sleep obscuring the bedside clock. He shakes his head with violence. Repeats this. Finally, time straightens out. *Good Christ*— when had he last slept this late? Before Junior's birth, no doubt.

Vic leaves Heather sleeping. Usually, she'd be up by now. But he didn't possess the energy for questions. Waking her would mean breakfast and small talk and that ominous look in her eye as he tried to say goodbye. Any depletion of what gas he has left, he knows, would ground him at home. Indefinitely. And so, he limps off to the front door, to his truck in the drive, and toward Elvis's and Jesus's trailer in Pond Eddy. With no music on and the windows down, the humid air pushing into the cab around him.

Vic's exhaustion follows him down the road through the onion fields, spreading a dreamy weirdness over everything while he drives, undulating the corrugated black dirt, draining the blue from the skies.

Outside the small aluminum trailer, he lays on the horn once. Then, a few more times. Until a pair of vultures startle from the faded satellite dish affixed to the roof of the trailer. There's no light in the windows, as far as he can see. No shadows. Yet he keeps honking. Eventually, he steps out of the truck to rattle the front door with his knocking and peers through the gaps in the sheets hung over the windows.

Then he repeats the process again. Because was that a prone body beneath the blankets? A whisper he heard from the bathroom? "Wake up in there! Look alive!" he says. But Elvis and Jesus refuse to surface, and he can sense the workday slipping away.

All the windows are open, a hot breeze blowing through them carrying the stench to Vic, who stands in the gravel driveway. From the diamond-plated box flush-mounted into the bed of his truck, he removes his trusty crowbar. A small sledgehammer that's been rounded down from years of use. A pair of knee pads whose hard plastic shells have degraded and cracked. If his helpers don't want to help, well, he's already got everything he needs, right?

Working crowbar between carpet and baseboard, Vic's knees crack arthritically and he can feel the blood pooling down into his sagging jowls. At this angle, the headache returns at once. Knifes at him with the accelerating, sharp pulse of his heart. He rips upward, and the sensation is like a muscle tearing. Sweat prickles and creeps throughout his scalp.

With each movement, he hisses, cursing through his teeth. He keeps working. A painful rhythm develops now. After a minute or so, he manages to peel up an edge of the carpet. A couple of inches, not much. *Must be hung up on a stubborn staple*, he thinks with a shake of his head. *Rusted in with age.*

Dizzied, he returns to the armchair. Was it *really* the Polaroids that scared Elvis and Jesus off? he wonders. Or had they decided to work with a younger developer with the future in mind? Or worse—had they received a scolding call from his wife? The brownish stain at his feet stares back at him, as if readying itself to answer these questions.

Vic gathers enough of himself to return to the edge of the carpet he's worked up. On hands and knees, he pulls and strains, ignoring the sharp ache in his lower spine. Until—*eureka!*—the staple finally gives, freeing another small segment of carpet, beneath which he discovers exactly what he'd been hoping for: wide oak boards, a floor that will gleam and ripple once he's sanded and polyurethaned them.

He might've whooped aloud with joy had Elvis and Jesus not walked in just then. Or who he thinks to be them at first—because as he looks up from their work boots to their dirty blue jeans, he notices shotguns and orange hunting vests. Beards. Two gnome-like men, paradoxically young and ancient-looking. Twins? Quite possibly. Two inbred killers straight from central casting.

"You the cops?" says one.

"Owner," Vic says. The air thins as he stands. "My wife and I."

"Owner?" says the other, taller than the first, if only by a little. He prods open a bedroom door with the nose of his shotgun. He wrinkles his nose. "God, it smells like death in here."

"What'd you do with Eugene's stuff?" the shorter one says.

Vic dusts off his hands on his jeans, preparing for a handshake that doesn't come. "Okay, I'll bite, whose stuff?" he says.

"Eugene's," says the taller one. "Our uncle. He ran a lucrative entertainment business and left us everything after he died."

"Left us the lodge, too," says the shorter one.

Vic laughs at this, eyeing the crowbar on the floor at his feet. His revving heart beats a tremor he fails to keep out of his voice. "You must be referring to the wad of hundreds I found. Your Uncle Eugene happen to have a last name, then?"

The shorter one looks to the taller one. "Same as ours."

"Which is?"

"Nice try, old man," the shorter says. "Now more about that wad of hundreds."

"Don't forget about the gold bars. But more on that later—what else was it your beloved Uncle Eugene left you again?" he says. "This uncle whose last name you don't even know?"

"Here. This," says the other one, the taller, prodding still with his shotgun. Another door, another empty room. The floor creaking as they pass from room to room, searching. Their muddy boots tracking across the oblong stain in the floor as they crowd the hunting lodge with their animal bodies.

"Our dear, sweet, enterprising uncle," the shorter says. He sniffs and wipes at his nose with the back of his large hand, like a child might.

Vic smirks at the absurdity of these twins. This problem that might require him to use his crowbar in a way he's never needed to in all his years of foreclosures and flips. One that'd waited, all these years, to find him all alone. And what's more: Suddenly, he trusts himself to do so. He's been waiting for this moment his entire life. "I assure you I threw out that illegal smut you're looking for," he says. "Consider your Eugene bankrupt. My wife is still debating whether the cops need to be called. Come to think of it, she's just down the road looking for service."

The taller shrugs. "Road seemed clear when we walked in."

"And as far as this smut? I can't say I know what you're talking about," the shorter one says. He stops his searching for the moment and stands there with the shotgun under his arm, not exactly pointing at Vic, but close.

"I think you might."

"Might be you're fixing up the wrong house. Maybe you bought the one next door. Everything looks the same out here." He shifts, the muzzle of the shotgun passing over Vic briefly.

He laughs. "There's no next door out here."

"Nothing but woods and nature's violence," the taller agrees just as the shorter places his foot over the crowbar—still within Vic's reach, if he just moved fast enough to take the shorter twin by surprise. But the shorter twin's sunken eyes hide which way he's looking.

"Seems like all that stuff you threw out is worth something," says the taller twin. "Seems to me you owe us some compensation."

"Owe you?" Vic says, seeing a different type of opening now. "I'll tell you a secret: I've remodeled countless homes and fixed them up and sold them for a profit. I eat mold for breakfast and lead for lunch. Asbestos for dinner. I've been chasing success for almost eighty years. I've provided for my family. And the one thing I've learned is the only way to make money is to earn it." He licks his lips, tasting copper. "So, I'll tell you what," he continues.

"You seem like good boys. Help me get this carpet up and I'll pay you five hundred bucks."

"Jesus wept," the shorter one says, then pauses to whisper up to the other. Or maybe it's the taller doing the whispering—one inbred killer to another.

The floor must be uneven, Vic thinks. Another thing he adds to his mental punch list, even now. "Five hundred each," whichever one it was says, and takes his foot off the crowbar. "And we want to see the money."

Vic writes out a check, says he'll sign after they've rolled the carpet up and hauled it into the bed of his truck. "I said money," the shorter says. "The green stuff."

"Take it or leave it," Vic says. "If it bounces, come back. I'll be here working. You'll know where to find me."

"That could be fun," the taller says.

"A laugh riot," the shorter says. "Not to mention, we've been meaning to get that carpet out of here anyway. Ever since our poor, beloved Uncle Eugene died. That sweet man. If we're ever going to fix this place up, that sinister fucking carpet has got to go."

Everyone forces a laugh at this—because, beneath their collective focus, suddenly, the carpet seems to stare back at them, as if listening. Seems to momentarily swell and release a noxious breath in the heat and glare at them through each of its matted and crusty fibers.

The possible twins remove their orange vests, pop the slugs from their shotguns, and lay them on the hearth of the soot-covered fireplace.

"You really threw out Eugene's collection?" the shorter says, like they're buddies now.

"You mean poor old Uncle Eugene?"

Another laugh. Then the possible twins carry the armchair outside as if it's light as a pillow. They remove the smashed television and the moldering coffee table. The carpet clear now, they then begin clawing at the edge Vic worked up with the crowbar, tearing it up fast and easy, hissing through their teeth each time the crowbar works up another length.

Yes, Vic thinks, as the carpet peels away, folds further over itself to hide that hideous stain. After a buff and sand, a little polyurethane, the floors will shine like a frozen brook. *Oh baby*—the visions are coming fast and sudden now: Kitchen cabinets blossom, new appliances gleam, the dusty air clears. A breakfast nook in the corner, something Heather would insist upon. An accent wall color no one would've conceived of that, even so, completely jibes. When they close the sale, he'll ballroom waltz her around the shiny hardwood floor. He'll whisk her away, anywhere she wants to go.

The carpet is up and rolled in the yard. Some of the smell taken with it. Most, in fact. Gone. His headache already receding in its absence. His vision returned. The twins have done in fifteen minutes what would've taken Vic days to do alone.

The possible twins agree to work up the remaining carpet staples for an additional two hundred bucks. From the edges, they move inward, prying the staples with cat's paws Vic grabbed from the truck. Crawling on hands and knees toward the center of the room, where the reeking stain had worked its way through the carpet and into the hardwood.

They work at such a rate that Vic might consider hiring them again, despite his better judgment. He stands to the side and watches them, pondering the oblong stain. "How did your Uncle Eugene die, if you don't mind me asking?" he finally says.

An exchange of glances. "Thyroid cancer."

"In the hospital."

"Surrounded by family and holding the hand of the only woman he'd ever loved," the shorter says.

Vic points. "You sure he didn't die right there on the floor?"

The possible twins seem to see the fetal stain for the first time: resolving into the shape of him, their supposed uncle, curling into death. The two clear patches that must've been from his shoes, the canvas and leather soaking up his bodily fluids like a sponge. Up there: Were those his fingers? And is that where the sap of his brain leaked out? Do you see there, and there? And there? Lookit now.

Vic continues like this, talking and pointing. Until the color leeches from the small revelations of face above their dense beards. The possible twins: suddenly reduced to little boys, no longer potentially ancient or feral men. Afraid, he realizes, as they begin to see their lie. That this residue, this human-shaped stain, is what became of the evil man that peddled smut and snuff out here. Nothing left but dried blood and bile.

"How about you go get the sander from my truck," Vic says, staring at the stain, his vision transporting him back into the realm of the house-that-will-be. And when he looks back up, the shotguns and orange vests are gone, the two men run off with them. Fled. He laughs at this, at these little boys posing as demons of the woods.

He drags the industrial sander inside himself, heart still working hard inside his chest, but powerfully now, his energy restored by the clarity of his vision and his brush with death. It's the charge of the same magic he's always felt on renovations, only stronger. He hauls the generator near the front door, plugs in the sander.

Then he yanks the generator's pull start until it coughs and chortles to life.

Eddies kick up around him as the sander skates across the floor, spits sparks like fireworks from staples the twins neglected. The stain being slowly eaten up, ground away into a yellow, drifting ghost.

Vic isn't wearing a respirator. He's probably breathing in all manner of harm. He knows this would displease Heather, if she knew—or most likely she *does* know. In fact, she's probably experiencing a jolt this very moment in the garden, he thinks with a smile. He can see her now. The surprised look on her face as she incorporates this death with him, as it wafts up to her via the fragrance of the enormous rose she's pruning. He can see her worried expression breaking and turning warm for him. Affectionate almost. Unmistakable now with yearning. Unable to help this. He sucks at the gritty air so she can taste it better with him. Feel that old thrill again, feel what's been missing. To strike the same beautiful note that she's been trying to muffle.

He's laughing until the dust catches inside his throat. Then he's coughing. Hacking with booming rattles that force him to his knees. With a violence he wouldn't wish on anyone, above all Heather. Who, in these final moments, he can't help but picture keeling over with him. With him as she'd always been, he understands with astounding clarity. Now on her side in the garden. Now on this hardwood floor, too. Riding the currents that flow through him into her. Buffering and guiding him, not chastising for not listening. Just loving him, selflessly. Their thudding hearts and seizing legs syncopated, spinning their horizontal bodies. In circles that slow, slow, slow—

REDISTRIBUTION OF A FAMILY MAN

Then Vic Greener—husband, father, friend, actor, playwright, underwear model, house painter, carpenter, landlord, seventy-five-year-old serial purchaser of foreclosed houses—dies from what the coroner will later deem a heart attack while sanding clean the hardwood floor of a haunted hunting lodge out in Pond Eddy.

His heart stops. Then the blood settles in the wells of his body. His body heating toward room temperature, which, at the time of death, happens to be over one hundred degrees Fahrenheit. As his brain continues dredging up Frankensteined memories: the netting of a tadpole from the murk of a pond morphs into the crunch of cold apples, into freshly cut grass that smells faintly of cilantro. A pale hand with red nails raking through black dirt. Then, the fluid glide of a paintbrush into the sound of the tongue twisters he once honed as an actor. His wife, Heather's, lips on the curve of his ear while the headboard knocks. The shrilling of his newborn son. A randomness, he perceives with a razor-sharp acuity that stuns him. Kills him. Sends him off. Until, finally, the montage snaps away into infinity and his jaw opens slowly, like a flower inviting sun.

Like this, Vic lies there. For hours. In the center of the partially sanded floor, the bottled heat of the hunting lodge fogging at the windows while outside, the generator continues running, its blue exhaust curling up into bluer skies. The industrial sander is still locked on, attempting to finish the job Vic started, drifting around in erratic circles, bumping into walls, scuffing them with its rubber grip handle, falling over and righting itself. Knocking once, twice, into Vic's prone body.

By midafternoon, the bag attached to this sander swells taut. And with nowhere to go, the excess grit begins escaping from anywhere it can: leaky gaskets and loosely stitched seams. In no less than a half hour, a hot patina lies thick on the partially sanded floor. And on Vic's body—in the creases of his ever-slackening face, his gray whiskers. The yawning hole of his drying mouth.

Meanwhile, the rogue industrial sander continues its elliptical journey. At this point, the gritted paper is completely gone. The metal orbital, exposed and cutting raw curves into the hardwood floor, sending vibrations through the floorboards that settle the dust deeper. Into Vic's face, the cracks of the floorboards. Sifting down into the darkness of the crawl space below—a tomb of moldy black—to disturb a brood of black widow spiders who've lived there, safe in their webs, for generations, unaware of the horrors occurring above them over the years.

Around sundown—when Heather expects Vic home for dinner—the generator gurgles, stops. The sander whirs to a halt beside Vic's body. The last of its dust settles to the ground like glitter in the sunlight, tinging the air gold—pink, even, coloring the flies that've begun to gather a neon crimson. The heat of the night: still undiminished, perhaps even hotter than the day's.

There are a few dozen flies or so, at first. But little by little, as more gases build and release from Vic's body, their numbers multiply into masses. As his stench continues to ring through the boiled air like a dinner bell, following the breeze, along with the wood particles, out the door into the moist yard. As inside the hunting lodge, the slackness of Vic's body turns to hardness. His fingers, elbows, and knees curve upward. And the flies continue.

* * *

The first carrion bird arrives—a large crow that's been perched in the oak tree for these past hours, sniffing at the sick-sweet particles streaming from the hunting lodge's wooden mouth. With a clatter of wings, this crow situates itself in the doorway. A shadow that moves like a metronome, deciding. Then, deeming the situation safe, the large bird takes a hop inside. Another. Until it's situated within reach of Vic's supine body.

Then, in one adroit movement, the crow hops onto his swollen chest. Its claws clenching the logo of the paint-speckled T-shirt over his stopped heart. His body farting under its weight. For a long moment, the crow stares into Vic's half-opened, glassy eyes. Then, a crimped smile brushes its blue-black beak, and the crow begins to clip at his face.

Meanwhile, a light breeze blows through the house with an off-key fluting sound, continuing to carry the smell of Vic's body into the wilderness beyond. Through the verdant leaves and wildflowers and copses of trees, into the twilight above. Where a tornado of vultures has already begun forming, a swirling lung that belies its grumble with hope for the bacchanalia to come, homing in on Vic's final location: the brown speck in all that green, this hideous hunting lodge.

And soon, the whole committee descends to fill the trees. To hold their wings out in suspended applause, in an attempt to dry the high-altitude moisture from their feathers. One by one, they glide to the ground, hopping clumsily toward the promise of what they smell to hesitate briefly in the doorway. Before hopping inside and across the floor toward Vic's body with a wariness that diminishes with each new guest. Each braver than the one that came before.

* * *

The first wails startle them. Some carrion birds hop away—out the door and into the safety of the trees—before returning to Vic's body with elevated fervor once the sirens have faded. They jockey for position, rubbing their ancient wings against those of their feasting neighbors.

A half hour later, the sirens return, pass again. But this time the feasters remain unfazed, filling their bellies with Vic's still-hot flesh in the piping sauna of the hunting lodge while the trills of pleasure bounce off the cramped walls and they gulp back another scrap of him.

The police keep calling Heather like she'd suddenly remember the hunting lodge's address or have some other tip to offer that'd set them in the right direction. "The overgrowth is so thick this time of year," they keep repeating to her. But Heather truly doesn't know the address and can't find any of his paperwork anywhere. No, she doesn't know someone from the county offices they could get on the phone this time of night. Not on a Friday, anyway. Only knows what she told them: the name he uttered before he started repairs: Pond Eddy, a hunting lodge.

"Probably, he went out for a beer," one officer tells her.

"Probably, he'll pull into your driveway any minute," another says.

But, in truth, Heather already knows what's happened, has seen this too many times these past years—her husband dying or dead inside a tomb of his own making.

"I hope you're right," she says.

When the police arrive—when they finally find the nearly imperceptible thinness of foliage that marks the driveway's start—the slamming doors start the vultures parading out the dark doorway into the fading light, hopping like crazed jesters across the slushy yard where, lethargic and sated, they struggle to take flight. The necrotic smell that's been absorbed inside their feathers radiating about the police-crowded yard.

One officer begins retching. Another crosses himself. Another glances at the servicelessness of his cell phone with a sudden stab of fear, thinking to call his wife—because there's no mistaking what awaits them in there: the dead old man and his jackhammered body. A pulverized human doll.

They approach the hunting lodge already drenched in sweat, with the same wariness of the earliest carrion birds. Stopping and starting again. Taking turns in the doorway to glance at the body through the dusk-lit nebula of dust. They gather themselves and return, stepping closer now, opening windows to release the fetid heat from the room, to no effect.

In Vic's truck, a box of dust masks is discovered and distributed. Voices muffled, the cops then say things behind the masks like: "How does something like this happen? And so quickly? Have you ever seen anything like this in all your life?"

Their feet squish in their hot, wet boots.

After a while, one of these voices calls for a body bag. By now, squad cars choke the yard and driveway, a growing audience. The blue and red of their service lights strobe against the cracked clapboard and along the quarter-mile stretch of potholes and gravel to the county highway, to that near imperceptible entrance. This is what now guides Heather toward the scene from her car, down the strobing tunnel of trees.

The first officer who spies her (the one who can't stop crossing himself) doesn't seem to comprehend her presence. To him, she's a ghost, an aberration. At any second, she might recede, in her white summer dress, back into the dark woods beyond the foggy yard, into folklore and legend. When she asks him what's happened, he takes a few seconds to wipe his brow as the police lights dance over him, before barking over his shoulder at the hunting lodge: "Sarge!?"

Instead of waiting to meet this *Sarge*, Heather walks past the officer, her sandaled feet sloshing through the soupy grass and her shadow strobing against the sloughing paint of the hunting lodge—her husband's final project. Which, now as she appraises it, appears every bit as horrifying as she imagined. Worse, really: the bristly hedges, the crooked shudders. The caving roof and drooping soffits. The damp, mosquito-friendly yard. She almost laughs at his blasphemy, his broken impulse to provide.

Like this, the sergeant finds her. He stands beside her and removes his ten-gallon hat. And after a deep breath, he begins telling her what she already knows: that her husband's inside, dead from what appears to be a heart attack. That the heat had accelerated the natural processes, and he'd been set upon prematurely by vultures. That the EMTs are currently in there preparing to transport the body. Maybe she shouldn't stick around. Maybe she doesn't want to remember him like that. "If there's any loved ones you can call?" he says.

Heather thanks him, insists that he returns to his business, that she'd like to be alone now. He cocks his head at this, studies her a moment before leaving her to stand there trying and failing to catch the future her husband saw in the lodge.

"The lodge beyond the lodge," as Vic would say. *Would've* said, she corrects.

The officers keep glancing at her while they work. The blanched fear of their blue-and-red faces grows inside Heather also, as she stands, realizing that, no, there is no hunting lodge behind this hunting lodge. Not this time. Nothing between the mold and moss and dank except his forever upward striving.

Something she could've told him at first glance, if she'd only looked. An omen every bit as obvious as this heat.

Heather calls Junior and recounts the events directly. Says what needs to be said. "No, this isn't some story I've concocted," she says. He really thinks she'd make this up? Like some sick joke? He falls silent on the other end, then a short burst of laughter. "You're serious?" he says.

"I'm serious," she tells him. "Really, I am," she says, and another silence stretches so long this time she thinks the call's been dropped. Then Junior's voice returns to her, as businesslike as her own, to say what you might expect—that he's sorry, so sorry, he'd always feared something like this. That he'd come as soon as possible to help her make all the necessary arrangements, figure out what to do about the properties, the house, the assets. He assumes she doesn't want to keep living in that desolate, old house all alone, after a tragedy like this. She'll come live with him and his wife.

But she surprises him: "No way in hell," she says.

By the time Junior arrives with his very pregnant wife, Heather has the table on the patio set with lunch: a steaming root roast with an enormous cauliflower, deep purple potatoes, and oblong carrots. They sink their forks into it politely, taking tentative sips of lemonade between bites as they discuss what needs to be done: the calls to the funeral parlor, the newspapers for his obit, the few relatives he had that are still alive. Acquaintances, friends from a distant past.

After the wake, the funeral, once his pregnant wife has retired to his childhood bedroom for the night, Junior and Heather sit at the kitchen table, drinking tequila on ice. The crystal glasses: cold and jingly in their hands as, through the window, the summer night knits a pure cacophony—a cross-hatching of steady madness.

And it's here, after a couple of refills, a comment or two about the whirlwind of the past few days, that Heather first mentions the hunting lodge. Asks what Junior thinks they should do with the property: "No one will buy that heap in the shape it's in," she says.

Junior falls silent, offended that his mother would think of business the day they'd buried his father in the ground. Would think he'd upend his life to make right the mistake of his father's final project. Before the maggots have even wriggled free from the eggs in his father's coffin to begin the journey of picking clean his bones. He sips his drink again, and the rage passes. "Someone will have to fix it up, I guess," he says.

And so, the next day, Junior drives over to appraise the hunting lodge, turns down the throat of overgrowth and rocks and down the driveway's potholes, his truck rocking, the tools in the back clattering. The doubt swelling within him, tauter and tauter, with every inch he drives. He must've made a mistake, gotten his mother's directions wrong, turned down a fire road. Soon, he'll blow a tire, become stranded. Meet the same tragic fate of his father—until, finally, the hunting lodge rears up from the mound of earth. More horrific than he imagined:

Those hedges?

The roof and crooked shutters?

The wet, rutted lawn where the police tires got stuck spinning?

The way the air is polluted with the septic no doubt leeching up into the yard?

There appeared to be no logic to glean at all.

Later, sitting at the kitchen table, Junior conveys this to his mother, laughs about it, really—that *this* would be his father's final act. This ghastly structure. A horror movie set. What was he even thinking? As far as hiring contractors, Junior wouldn't even know where to begin. They'd all just laugh at him or quote him an inordinate sum. And Heather's laughing, also. An infectious sound that sets her son laughing harder at the ridiculousness of it all.

Yet, every day thereafter, Junior stands in its gravel driveway, unable to write the hunting lodge off as a useless investment. No matter how hard he tries, he keeps hoping to discover his father's plans hidden somewhere within himself: the steps he might have broken down into smaller tasks, into these manageable bites with which he would've made his meal. His father's usual way of taking things, one day at a time.

He opens his notebook and writes: *Straighten the shutters, mend the drooping soffit, the roof. Trim the hedge. Finish sanding and staining the hardwood floor. Tape the corners, paint the walls . . .*

For a long time his pen doesn't stop.

In this way, slowly, over the next weeks, the lodge begins emerging for him, like a ritual offering. Piece by piece, sentence by sentence, Junior works to revive the thing. Ticking off each box, always opting for what's reasonable, not throwing money unnecessarily at the renovation. Like he thinks his father might have done.

At the end of the week, Junior says goodbye to his mother while she weeds in the garden. "I'll be back as soon as I can to get the hunting lodge moving," he says. And she smiles without looking up from the black dirt to watch him go—because she understands completely: that his wife deserves to have their baby in the privacy and comfort of their own home.

It's a future he drives off into without much thought: a healthy birth and a stoic little baby, a girl, who cries very little. Whose wrinkled face, he notices, tends to track toward the window in her nursery whenever possible. Toward the oak tree outside. At times, even mimicking the birds that sing there sometimes—or so he likes to pretend.

But in the back of his mind, the hunting lodge remains. Winter approaches, and the snow and ice are certain to make further renovations more tedious, more difficult in the long run. Really, he should return to do what he can. And so, in late fall, he does, bringing the whole family, in fact, to stay at his mother's house each weekend. So he can tentatively meet with carpenters and roofers, plumbers for prices. Then, after receiving their estimates and running numbers, to meet with no one at all, after deciding to tackle the renovations alone.

In the yard, through the doorway, he learns to take comfort in the smallest sounds: the gentle swish of leaves, the caw of crows, the shotguns that blast through the woods. The buzz of his drill in the hand, the swirl of his sander. The knocking of his hammer. Alone at the hunting lodge, he trims the evergreens back in hopes of drying the yard. He shapes the hedges. He shines the hardwood floors until they spit his blurred reflection back at him. In a poetry that he can't stop himself, at times, from writing down.

More and more, his mother stops by to help him. His wife and daughter, too, sometimes. But mostly just his mother. To deliver supplies he needs or to deliberate on what will be required going forward. Then, when spring comes, to weed the blackened garden beds and chop back the hedges. To tame the unruly lawn. To plant flowers that, come next summer, his mother swears, will complete the hunting lodge's revival, with pops of blue, purple, and brilliant yellow.

List of Images

Acknowledgments

Thank you Dad, my first editor and art friend. And thank you Mom, for telling me stories in the car.

Thank you to my perfect family: Caitlin, Wesley, and Meadow, for all your love.

Thank you Ben Schrank and Deborah Ghim, for believing in this novel.

Thank you David Ryan, for everything along the way.

Thank you Sean Williamson and Ashley Mayne, for always being there.

Thank you Halley Parry, for putting the work in.

Thank you Ashton Politanoff, Ben Samuels, JT Price, Evan Fleischer, BR Yeager, Frederick Barthelme, Derek White, Nathan Dragon, and Raegan Bird for publishing early chapters of *Foreclosure Gothic*.

Thank you Jon Huberth, Lynne Tillman, Rav Grewal-Kök, Jaclyn Gilbert, David Hollander, Nelly Reifler, Lincoln Michel, Nathan Dragon, Jon Lindsey, Sean Thor Conroe, Tracy O'Neill, Zain Khalid, Gabriel Smith, Bud Smith, Timothy O'Rourke, Mari Juliano, Eamon McBride, and anyone else who helped this novel.

ABOUT THE AUTHOR

Harris Lahti's short stories have appeared in *BOMB, New York Tyrant, Ninth Letter, Southwest Review, Forever Magazine*, and elsewhere. He cofounded Cash 4 Gold Books and edits fiction for *FENCE*. For a living, he paints and renovates houses in New York's Hudson Valley. Visit harrislahti.com.